MY DRAGON LOVER

Broken Souls 5

ALISA WOODS

Cover by BZN Studio

ISBN: 9798637082209

My Dragon Lover (Broken Souls 5)

None of this is real...

Not the severed head in the alley.

Not the men who think they're dragons.

All of it is some bullshit cosplay gang war.

Only I'm stuck in the middle.

And if the "good" side is crazy, the "bad" side is downright murderous.

So I'll stick with the intense guy who's my private security for now.

Just until I know Grace is safe. And Daisy too.

Then I'm getting the hell out of this place.

Because I can't afford to lose my job over this. Not after everything that's happened...

Jayda wants nothing to do with men who play dress-up. Ree's not there to change her mind—his job is to protect her body, not win her heart. But keeping her safe means convincing her to stay, and he knows just how to keep a woman in his bed. But it's a dangerous game... one his heart is certain he'll lose.

My Dragon Lover is a steamy dragon shifter romance that'll heat up the sheets with love and warm your heart with dragonfire.

ONE

Jayda

AN ANNOYINGLY BEAUTIFUL MAN IS KEEPING ME from leaving.

I only came to the gallery to see Grace's opening of the exhibit—to support her in re-enacting her great-grandmother's experience of the internment camps—but she left over an hour ago with a boy who's in love with her. They're probably having hot sex in the warehouse in back. Which I fully support—anything to help Grace move past the trauma of what we both went through. Our friend Daisy is still recovering, stuck in a hospital bed in a coma, but Grace isn't. She should grab every good thing in life and run with it.

"Do you think this barbed wire is real?" The beautiful man is peering at the razor wire strung around the walls, encircling the photographs that depict Grace's great-grandparents' internment.

"Probably."

"I mean, it looks real."

"Yep." *Kill. Me. Now.* I manage not to say that out loud. This is one of those conversations that consists of literally nothing and never ends. *Vacuous.* I'm not a snob—small talk has its place—but there's just no *there* there with this guy.

"Seems kind of dangerous, though."

"I guess?" I edge away.

"But it's like… *rusty.*"

I almost can't contain my exasperated sigh, so I just keep quiet. I can't figure out where this guy fits in the constellation of rich and important people crowding the gallery all around us. Grace's family is made of money, and the people here are the glitterati of New York City mingling with the old-money class. Not too many hedge-funders, the kind I work with every day, but a gaggle of *artistes,* actors like Grace. This guy who's occupying my time and personal space is goofy and gorgeous—vaguely European, light gray eyes, sharp-cut cheekbones, and built like he'd be fine to ride. Maybe he's one of those actors who get by on looks alone—empty-headed but serious eye candy. Which reminds me I haven't had sex in a long time. No action since my ex, which is a very depressing thought. Maybe some hot sex is just what I need to move forward too, and this delicious piece of man flesh before me could be just the thing.

Only he's not giving off the right vibe. Or maybe I've been out of the game too long.

I lick my lips. "I'm sorry, what's your name again?"

He smiles. "Aleks." He takes two flutes of champagne from a passing server and holds one out for me.

"Thanks." I take it and sip. Is Aleks down for sex? Why else would he be holding me socially hostage in this gallery filled with people more glamorous than me? It's not for the scintillating conversation. The awkward between us is verging on painful. Sex would be tolerable only if we didn't talk.

He's smiling, but it's stressed. He gives a serious nod to the barbed wire. "I think it's real. Seems like everything here is... real." He winces, and I barely restrain myself from rolling my eyes. He could easily move on to someone else, but he keeps stringing this along. Why? Is it because I'm the only black person in this super-white Chelsea crowd, despite this being an installation on Japanese-American history? I'm used to being the only black woman at work—and all the headwind that comes with that—I don't need to deal with any more of that nonsense, even for sex. If Aleks has some kind of interracial fetish, he's in for some disappointment pie.

That's it. I'm done with whatever this is.

"Well," I say dramatically, glancing at the time on my phone like I've just discovered it exists. "I really should get going." I have piles of work waiting for me back at the office, anyway. And I've done what I came here to do.

"So soon?" He glances over my shoulder. "I hear they're bringing out food soon. You don't want to miss that!"

I lift the champagne flute. "This is all I need." I slam it back, then hand the empty glass to a wide-eyed Aleks. He immediately swaps it for his, another bid to keep me engaged. For what possible reason, I honestly don't know.

I sigh as I take the fresh glass. "I'm not that easy to get drunk, Aleks." I need to find my exit from this, *now,* but I drain the champagne anyway. It's too much bubbly at once, and my eyes water. I dab at the corners and try to blink the tears away. I've got full office makeup on, and I don't want to mess it up. While I'm trying to recover, Aleks's expression transforms from awkward weirdness to massive relief. *"Thank God,"* he says under his breath, but he's not talking to me. He's signaling someone over my shoulder.

I twist to look, still fighting the blur in my vision. Two men are working their way through the crowd toward us. One has his gaze locked on me like a heat-seeking missile, and the *intensity* of it captures me. He's *rough*—eyes hard and dark, scruff of beard on his face, body moving with a power so solid people just flow out of his way like water. He has the same European look as Aleks, but there's nothing goofy or *pretty* about this man—he's just pure iron will, focused on me like I'm a pool of water, and he's dying of thirst.

I scarcely breathe as he stalks closer. My whole body is suddenly radiating heat. He stops six feet away, like there's an invisible barrier holding him back, and consumes me with his eyes instead.

"You made it," Aleks says with obvious relief.

Only then do I tear my gaze away from the intense *maleness* of this dark-eyed man and check out the one who came with him. He's gorgeous, the same European hotness, only this one I know.

"Niko." My voice is flat. *"Shit."* My heart leaps to full panic. I shoot a look at Aleks, seeing him anew. And the intense man who's still heating my skin with his gaze. They're all together, all part of the same group of *assholes* who play like they're secretly dragons. They're part of some cult—some gang of cosplayers, rivals to the ones who kidnapped Grace and Daisy and me. Kidnapped and *tortured* us.

I step back. "Stay away from me." It's a whisper. There's nowhere to go. The gallery is too crowded. I barely have room to fight, even if I could. *Three of them.* But we're in public. They can't take me, not without half of the city's elite as witnesses.

Niko steps forward. "Jayda, you need to come with us."

"The hell I do." I shrink back further, bumping into a passing server and nearly causing a disaster of spilled drinks and ruined cocktail dresses. Niko is their leader—the one who tried to sell me the whole story about their "hidden dragon society." The one who wanted all three of us to stay and fulfill whatever fantasy they had about rescuing us from the freaks who tortured us. Grace's hot new boyfriend, Theo, is one of them—I should have known he would bring the others, eventually.

"Jayda, *please.*" Niko steps closer, pleading, but not like he's going to force me. Because he can't. We're in public. Aleks has dropped back behind him. The other one, with the laser-focused smolder, is holding back too.

My panicky heart settles a little. I still have the upper hand here. "I told you before…" I straighten and smooth down my tailored jacket. "I want nothing to do with your games." Then I realize… and dart a look toward the back door. "Where's Grace?"

"She's safe." Niko glances around, keeping his voice low. "Theo's taken her to a safehouse. Which is what we need to do for you, right now. This place isn't safe for you."

"What the fuck are you talking about?" I've matched his low tone, speaking through my teeth. If I have to yell for help, I will. But Grace's parents are here, and I don't want them freaked out by whatever bullshit this is. It's all fantasy with these guys. Some elaborate game they're playing, only the others, the ones who kidnapped us, are deadly serious. I want nothing to do with any of them, but these I can handle—I got them to leave us alone before. I can do it again. I just need to make sure Grace isn't tangled up in their games, then I'll get

7

the hell away from them. I fumble to retrieve my phone from my pocket and quickly text Grace, *You okay?*

Niko's peering at me while I'm typing. "She's probably shook up right now."

I look up. "Why are you even here? Can't you just leave us alone?"

He tips his head toward the back. "We came because Grace needed us. Come outside. I'll show you why."

I give him a pinched look. "You're completely cracked if you think I'm leaving with you."

He grimaces. "Jayda… we're not the ones you need to be afraid of." He dips his head and speaks even more softly. "Do you remember what I told you before? About the *Vardigah?*"

"I don't care about your games." But my throat closes up hearing the name. That's what he called the freaks who kidnapped us. I've put all that behind me. Grace is moving on. I don't need to think about those damn chairs they put us in or the probes they put to our heads… the screams and the pain… I've had enough of that in my nightmares. Why isn't Grace texting back? I stab at my phone, avoiding Niko's questioning expression. *Grace, I need to know you're okay.*

"Theo has her in a safe place," Niko says softly. "They came for her, Jayda."

My head whips up. "You said they couldn't find us."

"They did." His expression is grim but calm.

"But... Theo said..." I suddenly can't look at him. My gaze darts all over the room. Are the Vardigah here? They can't be. They'd stand out with those ridiculous pointed ears and ugly faces. But if those were just masks—

"We need to move you," Niko says. "And we need to do it *now.*"

I stare at my phone. No response. I look up at Niko. "You said Grace is safe."

He nods. "And we're moving Daisy, too. *Please,* Jayda. You're endangering the whole gallery by staying here." He's stepping back now, sweeping his arm toward the back door.

I'm frozen in place. I don't want any of this to be real. None of it *is* real, not in the sense they say. There's no magic. No fucking dark elves who like to kidnap and torture women who are the soul mates of the dragon men. None of that shit is real. What's real is what happened to us. The pain and the trauma. Somehow, for reasons I haven't even tried to understand, the three of us—Grace, Daisy, and

9

me—are trapped in some war between these crazy groups of people. And if these Vardigah assholes really are back, I know the side I need to be on to survive.

And sometimes surviving is all you can do.

"What do I need to do?" I ask Niko. My voice catches in the middle, so I clear it. And try to quell the shaking in the pit of my stomach.

The relief softens his face. "Come with us." He leads the way toward the back, the same door Grace and Theo left through a while ago. Aleks and the other man, the intense one who's tracking me with *all* his attention, follow behind. We work through the crowd, then into the warehouse in back, but Niko heads straight for a door to the outside. It's night, probably almost eleven by now. The alley in back is dimly lit, mostly by the street-light down at the end. But as my eyes adjust...

Bodies. There are bodies in the alley. No, body *parts.* A severed head with pointed ears stares blindly from where it's rolled up against a dumpster.

"Oh, my God." My hand covers my mouth automatically. I curl over and brace the other on my knee, feeling like I'm going to be sick.

Niko blocks my view of the pieces and gently grasps hold of my shoulders to straighten me up.

"I'm sorry. But I didn't think you would believe us without seeing for yourself."

The intense guy is right behind Niko, breathing hard like he's ready to kill something.

Aleks is looking down the alley with disgust. "Go on," he calls to Niko. "I'll stay and clean up the mess."

Niko lifts his chin in acknowledgment then releases me. "You okay? We have a ride waiting." He tips his head down the alley, which means we're walking past the body parts and the greenish liquid spilled around them. *Blood.* It has to be. What the fuck? Is the weird light of the city at night playing tricks?

I breathe through my teeth to avoid the smell. "Let's go."

Niko leads, but the other man is close behind. They're hovering like they think I might keel over. I'm no wimp, but my stomach roils as we pass the headless body and stride the length of the alley. An Uber is waiting. Niko nods to the driver as we climb in. I guess he already knows where we're going, although I have no idea. All three of us—Niko, the other man, and me—squeeze in the back seat.

Niko turns in the seat to face me. "I need to ask a favor of you."

I snort a small laugh. This whole thing is insane. "Where are we going?"

"That's exactly it." He flicks a look to the man on the other side of me who seems to be trying to weld himself into the side of the car to avoid touching me. "We keep a safehouse here in the city, one the Vardigah don't know about, but we want to keep it that way. Do you remember when you left the hospice back at our lair?"

"No, I don't, actually." My tone is arch, driven by the rise of the small hairs at the back of my neck. *I don't remember.* Toward the end of the time we were held captive, I was passing out a lot. Then one time, I woke up in a hospital bed, apparently rescued from my torture cell by Niko and his band of demented dragon cosplayers. I found Grace and Daisy and demanded they release us. Which they did—we ended up back at Mount Sinai in the city—but the weird thing was I couldn't remember getting there.

"You don't remember because we drugged you." He says it with a tiny amount of apology that's nowhere near sufficient.

"Oh," I say. "So, I guess the *fuck you* I have screaming around in my head directed toward you and all your kind is long overdue."

A small smirk flashes across his face then disappears when he glances at the man next to me. I twist to give him a glare, so he knows I don't trust him either. None of them. His rock-hard expression seems directed at Niko, but it's probably a horrible mistake to be in a damn Uber with either of them going God-knows-where.

With a straight face, Niko says, "Fair enough. But we're going to need you to put on a blindfold, regardless."

"Excuse me?"

"I can't have you knowing where the safehouse is."

"The safehouse you want me to go to? *To hide in?*" My face scrunches up. What kind of fool does he think I am? "You want me to basically let you kidnap me."

He sighs. "It's for your protection and ours. If you, even inadvertently, tell people where you are, the Vardigah might find you. Honestly, we're not *at all* sure how they found Grace. And until we figure that out, we need to keep security as tight as possible. Think of it like witness protection." He digs into his jeans pocket and pulls out a black silk mask that looks like it belongs in a kinky pajama party.

"Please. Just put it on long enough for us to get there and get inside."

"You have got to be kidding me." I ignore his mask and stare forward at the Uber driver. He's a nervous-looking Indian man who probably didn't sign up for this shit either. I check my phone. Still no message back from Grace. I have only Niko's word that she's okay. But those Vardigah in the alleyway were no joke. Unless that was all staged. I just don't know anymore. I feel like I'm losing my damn mind, and that's *way* too close to how I felt in that cell. I still don't know how they did half their tricks. The torture was some kind of mind-fuckery, which made it even harder to keep everything straight. And to not lose hope. I would have been gone without Grace and Daisy to figuratively hold onto—they were the voices in the next-door cells that kept me sane. The Vardigah's mind probe was an electric rod or maybe a magnetic thing that somehow got inside my head and made it feel like my mind was melting. I've never been so scared in all my life. Not of the pain. Not of the creeps in their stupid costumes. *Afraid of losing my mind.* It's the only thing I've ever had—the only thing that's gotten me where I am—and I can *not* afford to lose that. And right now, Grace is tangled up with these dragon-fantasy guys, sucked back in by her hot boyfriend. Theo has her tucked away somewhere, and Niko's my only connection right now because she's not answering her texts.

Again. *Fuck, Grace, why aren't you picking up?*

I pull in a breath and blow it out. Sometimes, you do what you have to do. I snatch the mask from Niko's hands. "Fuck you for making me do this." I work on putting it on, and I manage to get it over my eyes, so now I can't see, but it requires tying in the back, and *fuck me*, but my hands are shaking. And my hair is *big*, a natural afro style I've been wearing ever since the Massive Flameout with my ex. Which makes it difficult to navigate getting the mask on. Without a word, the guy next to me takes the strings and ties them, not too tight, but snugly fitting, so the eye mask stays in place.

"Thank you," Niko says, probably to me, although I can't see anything anymore, so who knows. "We're almost there."

Now I wish I'd paid attention to where we were going. Toward Midtown, I think? Although I suppose that's the point—they don't want me to know. The Uber rolls to a stop. I hear traffic outside, but nothing to differentiate it from any other street in the city. Niko takes my hand and urges me out of the car. This is crazy. I'm wearing my office heels. I'm going to break my damn neck. They seem to figure that out quick because I've got one on each arm now, gently guiding me forward, telling me when to step up over the threshold of some door. They're both like rocks under my arms. The muscles on these guys are Olympic level. My kickboxing prowess might be awesome in the gym, but my momentary fantasy of fighting them off in the gallery was pure delusion. They're gentle, too— I'll give them that. I'm like a delicate package they're afraid they will break, judging by the way we nudge forward, one baby step at a time. I think we get in an elevator, a guess that's confirmed when the floor sways under me. I clutch for a second at their arms, but I'm not that unsteady. Just kind of freaked. When we step out of the elevator, everything is dead quiet. I didn't notice it so much before —the sounds of the street were still apparent on the first floor—but whatever floor we're on now must be way above the traffic. We step through one more door, and suddenly, they release me.

"You can take it off now." The voice is gruff. Must be the other guy, not Niko.

I fumble at the strings in back, but it's not like I'm the one who tied them in the first place. He moves behind me and takes over, one long pull that loosens the entire thing until it falls away. I don't know what I expect, but a crisp, modern, luxury apartment isn't it. The décor is very European, all clean lines and white-and-gray with natural woods. No windows, though, which is odd, given how upscale it is—probably as expensive as Grace's apartment only without the view. The two of us are standing in a great room with a towering ceiling, abstract art on the walls, and a small grouping of couches and chairs that look like a formal party of furniture.

Wait... "Where's Niko?" This place is big, but I don't remember hearing the door open again. I stop gawking at the apartment and turn to the guy whose name I still don't know. "And who the fuck are you?"

"My name is Ree." It's like I pulled some kind of admission out of him that he doesn't want to make. And that intense stare is back. What the hell? And where did Niko skip off to, leaving me all along with this dude who's sexy as hell but looks like he doesn't want to be here any more than I do.

"Just *'Ree'?* What kind of name is that?"

But my needling just makes him step closer in an intentional, fluid kind of way. Like he's stalking up to me, prepared for the fight, and supremely confident he'll be the victor. It sends a shiver down my spine—not fear but a cousin to that heat from before.

"My name is Vrakgar Alarie Beaumont Cendrillion."

I lean back. "Really." He has an accent under all that gruffness, but it's so subtle, I can't tell what it is. He's 100% serious about that ridiculous name.

"Yes." He's staring into my eyes like he wants to drill the meaning of that into me. I sense that invisible force field again, the one holding him back.

"Okay, whatever." I wave off his intensity because *Jesus*, that's more than I need right now. "Where the hell is Niko?" There's a hallway at the far end, leading away from the main room, but he couldn't have snuck off there so fast. One of two doors at the close end must be where we came in. "I don't know what you're thinking, Niko," I call out as I head toward the doors. He's got to be close by, he was holding me up ten seconds ago. "But I'm not hiding out in some apartment with tall, dark, and oddly-named here all night." As I reach the door, Ree is suddenly at my side.

"Niko's gone." Ree places his hand on the door like he's going to stop me from opening it.

I give him a pinched, unimpressed look. Then I step over to the other door and pull it open—there's an elaborate gourmet kitchen on the other side, but no Niko.

"He can't be *gone.*" But my heart rate is kicking up a notch. What's going on here? "He was just here." I return to the door Ree is physically blocking me from opening. I fold my arms and give him my best *I'm from accounting, don't mess with me* stare. "You gonna open that door before Niko escapes down the elevator, or do I need to remove your hand involuntarily?" It's a threat I can't back up, but maybe a bluff is all I need.

A flash of something like genuine fear crosses his face, but I can't believe it's real. I talk a good game, and I could take on someone who wasn't so incredibly solid and well-muscled, but there's nothing Ree-the-Vrakgar or whatever could possibly fear from me.

He slowly slides his hand off the door and steps back.

"I'm glad we understand each other," I say and pull open the door.

Then I stand there, in the threshold, stunned.

On the other side is a massive hall—at least twenty feet wide and a hundred feet long. It's made of giant blocks of stone, the kind you quarry and haul in and use to build castles, not apartments in the middle of the city. There's no elevator to be seen. But what's got my mouth dropped open and my heart trying to leap out of my chest are the *windows*.

Tall, skinny windows of leaded glass that let in the rosy light of the pre-dawn sun.

It's not morning. It's almost eleven o'clock at night. In New York City. Which this is definitely not.

The floor seems to sway under me. *"What the hell?"* I breathe and whirl on Ree. "Where the fuck are we?"

TWO

Ree

Bringing her here was a mistake.

The halls are filled with ghosts—memories I excised from my mind long ago. Only now, with Jayda standing on the stone pavers of my ancestral home, they've suddenly returned. Why did I instinctively bring her here? I could have picked any of the dozen apartments I keep around the world. This place is a scar, long grown over but still marring my soul, and I'm going to split it wide open again? *What the fuck, Alarie?* Did Jayda's beauty and presence just render you senseless? Or was it all the blood rushing to your cock that stopped the rational thought in your head?

"Where the fuck are we?" she demands.

"France." A vast, horrible mistake, I've already decided.

"What?" Her eyes are wide and *angry.* Power ripples off her and, *curse me*, I want to drag her back into the apartment and fuck my way out of this. But she's already turned away and stumbled into the south hall that looks out over the Dordogne River. "We are not in fucking *France!"* She yells it, defiant, into the empty hall, her hands fisted at her side. Her entire body is strung tight, and everything about her makes me clench with need. The strong curve of her calves. The deep brown of her skin. The trim waist above flared hips. Her tailored suit hugging her body makes me want to set it free in every possible way. I've felt that way all along—while I was rescuing her, unconscious, from the Vardigah, and all during my surveillance, tracking her movements, watching her from the shadows, making sure she was safe—but now, my fingers have brushed the cloud of her curls, and their softness has set off a rumble of desire that's wrecking me. I knew it would be bad. I sensed it the instant the witch connected us in that verdant meadow in the Irish countryside. I've been avoiding contact precisely because I knew my need for her would be insatiable —I would be a prisoner to it. I might survive giving

into that, but I've been in enough life-and-death situations to know when something can destroy you. When it has the power to tear apart everything you've carefully patched together. Jayda terrifies me, and there are few things on this earth which can do that.

Yet here I am, alone with her.

She's ready to flay me and toss me in the river. Well, not *me*, specifically. Any dragon within reach would do, I suspect. She wants nothing to do with us—she's made that clear—and she'd want even less to do with me, specifically, if she knew who I was. Or almost anything about me.

Jayda turns her anger to me, a finger pointed in accusation. "You drugged me. Again. I... somehow..." The heat of it wavers, her eyelids fluttering. She looks unsteady.

The urge to touch her is overwhelming. I sweep in and grab hold of her accusatory arm, giving her an anchor in a world that has to seem mad.

She shoves me away.

"It's disorienting." I can hear the tightness in my own voice. The *need*. "The teleportation fucks with your head." There's no sense trying to hide it now. I'd hoped to avoid this, certainly not reveal how we got here five seconds after we arrived, but a woman like her finds the truth with unerring speed. She *needs* the truth. I understand and respect that, given how many people lie to themselves all day long. "The blindfold was for you, not us."

"No." Her brow is scrunched up, her cheeks ashen, like she might be sick. "No more of your games."

I shrug. The reality of magic is the one truth she's still denying. That's her choice. I'm not here to change her mind—my job is to protect her body. "The jet lag is killer, even when the transport is instantaneous. It's still night in New York. You should go to bed." I wrestle actively with the part of me that wants to seduce her into it. I could wear down her resistance with an orgasm. Gain her compliance with three. Lose myself in the heat of her body. I have to shut my mouth to keep the watering from becoming drool.

That way lies danger, Alerie. Don't be a fool.

She just blinks. Once. Twice. Then she fumbles her phone out of her pocket and stares at it. "It's five in the morning." She shakes her head, then pivots on those heels that make her legs even longer, and strides to the closest window in the long line of them down the hall. Bracing both hands against the stone surrounding the glass, she stares out, eyes agog. I can see her chest rise and fall, her breath audible as I come up behind her.

The countryside is quiet in the early morning, the river slow and curved. The stone bridge stands silent across the water. Even the ducks are lazy in their float. It's why I come here, when the ghosts aren't roaming the halls—the pace is slow, the estate large, and I can retreat from the world a while. There's no place anywhere that is home, not any longer, but this comes closest.

"Or we could take a walk." I'm not sure I could stay out of her bed at this point. The garden is probably safer.

Jayda gives me a side-eye glare, then stabs at her phone. She taps something in and waits, but she's not getting the response she wants. Her groan of frustration goes straight to my cock. I grab hold of her wrist, which makes her eyes fly wide. I want to pin her to the rough stone wall, but I restrain myself, even though her skin is as alluringly soft as her hair. Instead, I simply point to the phone. "It's late in New York. Six hours time difference. No one's going to answer until the morning."

She wrenches her wrist from my hold, but I see the dilation of her eyes. The parting of her lips. *She feels it.* This connection or bond or whatever the fuck it is that we have as soul mates. Or maybe it's simply lust. I know the impact my body's presence can have—I use that effect often enough—and Jayda may be my undoing, but she's not immune to the call of the bedroom.

God help me. I *will* have her. Even if it destroys me. Knowing that won't stop me. A shiver runs through me, and I can't decide if it's fear or lust. But it distracts me enough that Jayda's backed away before I realize it.

"You did *not* teleport me to France," she insists from her space several feet away.

"No, I didn't. Niko did. He's the mated dragon, and only mated dragons can teleport. Like the Vardigah can. But you already knew that." I dip my head to peer into her eyes, which are still wide and slightly frantic. I know she remembers the torture—will she admit that nothing about that is explainable with physics as she knows it?

Her fear settles into seething. "I don't know how you did it. I don't know what…" She gestures at my estate all around us. "…what the fuck all this is. Or what trick you used to get me here. But I'm *not* staying. I'm not hiding out here, wherever this is. I've got a job. I can't go running around, playing your fantasy games—"

"It's Sunday morning, here in France. Saturday evening in New York. Surely, your job can wait until Monday."

This sparks even more fire in her eyes. "I don't expect you to understand—"

"This is for your protection." *This* argument, at least, is very familiar.

The fire builds to an inferno. "From *what?* The *other* assholes running around, playing games? How do I know that wasn't all faked? All some giant trick! Just to get me here and… and…" I hear the fear under the anger. The confusion and panic. That's familiar, too.

I hold out my hand. "Give me your phone."

"What?"

"Your phone… please."

I can practically hear her heart thumping. The indecision wars on her face. I wait. If she can't trust me with this, I'll have to seriously re-think my approach.

Slowly, hesitantly, she places her phone in my outstretched palm. I quickly pull up my website, the one I use for clients. Then I return it to her.

"I'm your protection detail." Private security. Mercenary. Special forces. I've done them all over the last hundred and ninety years of my adult life.

Cendrillion Security, Your Personal Solution to Global Security, blares from my website on her phone. I've spent the last decade making money by keeping rich assholes alive and safe. Or just their wives and daughters. Women who are their soft underbelly—women who rarely want private security intruding into their lives. Talking them into accepting protection is part of the job. I fuck them, too, but only the ones who aren't as monstrous as their husbands or fathers. Or if they're pretty enough for me to forget.

I have standards. Not many, but some.

Jayda's hunched up shoulders soften. She respects competence, as do I, and my resumé is fairly convincing of that. She looks up from the phone, measuring me anew with those intelligent brown eyes. "You've really done all these things?"

A smile tugs at my lips. "Which part don't you believe?"

She frowns at the phone and reads from it. "Ultra-high net worth individual, close security detail, Pinkerton, UK Division." She looks up. "Who were you guarding?"

"I can't say." I smirk. "But you've likely seen him if you watch movies at all."

She narrows her eyes. *"And* you worked for NATO's Ambassador in Kabul?"

"That was slightly more dangerous."

She lowers her phone. "This could all be made up, too."

I shrug. "Believe what you like. But I have the skills to keep you safe, Jayda. I've literally done this for a living my entire life. You don't have to believe anything else to know that I'm capable of protecting you and will disable, disarm, and if necessary *kill* anyone—*anything*—that tries to harm you." The only real danger to her is the Vardigah, and I would love to get my talons on one of them. Or ten of the bastards. I'm not foolish enough to wish they'd make an attempt—I don't want Jayda in that kind of situation or even witness to it—but I wouldn't be sorry if I found myself doing violence to Vardigah. Not with all they've done.

The tension in her body softens. Her eyes are luminous in the morning sun. It takes everything I have not to slip a hand into her hair, draw her in, and feast ... and not stop until both of us are shaking. *Her* definitely first.

"This is all... exhausting." But I can tell she believes me—at least the part she needs to. That she's safe with me.

"I know. You need to rest." I gesture back to the apartment, the small section of the estate that's thoroughly modern. My palms are itching to touch her again, and I'm once again wrestling with the part that wants to lead her to the guest room, close the door, and spend the next twelve hours indulging.

She's not moving. "I really need to know what day it is."

"Look at your phone."

She scowls at it. "Is it really Sunday? Is this part of the trick?" She mumbles it, then raises her gaze. "Look, it's really important. I *can't* miss this meeting I have on Monday." Alarm passes over her face. "I don't even have my computer! *Shit.*" She curls her hand around her phone and presses it to her forehead, closing her eyes briefly. "Oh, my God, this is a disaster."

"It'll be fine—"

She drops her hand and glares at me. "It will *not* be fine! You and your fucking cosplay gang war— you stole two weeks from me, weeks where I was fucking *locked up* and *getting tortured*—and that nearly cost me my job. And I *can't* lose this one, not again. You do not understand—"

"Okay. All right." My hands are up, placating. Because she's right. I barreled into this with no plan whatsoever. The moment I discovered she was in danger, I was laser-focused on whisking her away to safety. And then she was so mouth-watering in person, everything in me has short-circuited. *Get your shit, together, Alarie.* "Make me a list. Everything you need. I can get your computer and anything else. I'll have it here within hours. Meanwhile, you need to get some sleep. Rest up in case the worst happens, and we have to move again. I want you ready to decamp, portable, in case they find you. If they do, I'll fucking murder them where they stand. They will not touch you, I can promise you that. But it'll mean we have to move again, and you'll need to be well-rested, just in case. Deal?"

I can see her relax as I talk. Or maybe she's mirroring my calm. It helps to treat her like this—a client—rather than what she really is.

The other half of my soul.

I shove that thought aside as quickly as it forms.

"Deal." Her voice is quiet. Hushed. The ashen color in her cheeks is back. She steps toward the apartment and stops, giving me a weary look. "Just promise me it's not really Monday."

"It's really not Monday." I say it with the conviction of truth. She could look it up easily enough, but I have the feeling she's questioning her own perception of everything right now. And that's not okay. I need her steadier than that if she's going to comply with my directions—that's *essential* to keeping her safe. Especially given I don't know how the Vardigah are tracking her yet.

She nods and shuffles toward the apartment. Even exhausted and emotionally broken down, she has a certain sensuality in how she moves. I picture the muscles that must be under all that office wear. My fantasy skips ahead to her flexing that strength as she's riding me. Everything in me tightens as I follow behind, wrestling with the part that's already seeing her naked, spread before me.

I guide her to the guest bedroom. "There are nightclothes in the dresser." I keep the place well-stocked for all kinds of visitors. Or rather, the housekeepers do. "There's a pad of paper on the desk. Write down what you need and slip it under the door. I'll be nearby at all times. I'll stop back in a little while for that list and get to work on that while you rest." I've got a grip on the door frame, not allowing myself to step inside. The guest bedroom is really a suite—bed, sitting area, desk, computer, en suite bathroom—everything she needs. And there's plenty of room to not feel cramped.

I don't mention the cameras.

She's looking forlornly at the bed, a four-postered mahogany that's been well-used over the years, by me and an endless parade of bedmates. My mind conjures velvet ties around her ankles, each tethered to a different post.

I grip the door jamb harder. "All right?" The strain in my voice makes her look back.

"All right." It's resigned.

I close the door and get myself the hell away from that room. I tell myself I'll need to watch her closely to make sure the Vardigah don't track her and show up in her bedroom. It has the merit of being true. But I've got three separate fantasies of Jayda I need to work out of my system before I'll be fit for doing anything else... and with just my hand to do the job.

If I hurry, I can watch while she changes.

THREE

Jayda

I'M PINNED DOWN.

The bastards have hauled me to the chair again, and I'm pinned by those nightmare appendages, the ones that come up from below. Grace is here—somehow, the wall is transparent now, and she's banging on it and shouting, but I can't hear what she's saying. And it doesn't matter anyway because they've got the probe out, the one they put to my head, the one that tears apart my mind. I struggle and thrash, and my body splits open, gashes bleeding everywhere, but it doesn't matter, they don't stop. They press the crystal probe to my temple, and I open my mouth and scream and scream and scream—

"Jayda! Wake up!"

I gasp in air and bolt straight up. Someone has me, rock-hard grip on my shoulders, but I fight them and fight them. My scream is still echoing in

34

my ears, my throat hoarse from it, even though I know it was just a dream.

A nightmare.

I stop fighting. My heart is beating so hard, it spasms like I'm having a heart attack. I gulp in air, one gasp after another and another. My eyes finally focus on the man holding me.

Ree. "You're okay. You're safe." His voice is deep and strong, like an anchoring rock in a wild hurricane. He's on the bed with me. I think he climbed up to restrain me. "You just had a bad dream."

I nod because I can't speak—I'm still trying to calm my ragged breathing and pounding heart.

He releases me and backs off the bed. "I'll get you some water. Just stay there." He turns and sprints to the bathroom. I hear the water go on.

I blink and work my legs free of the tangle of sheets. Everything is shaking. The lightweight pajamas leave me chilled, and the stone floor is cold on my bare feet. I'm trying to stand by the time Ree returns with a cup of water.

He glares at me while holding the water out. "You don't take direction very well."

My hand shakes as I try to bring the water to my mouth.

"Hey." He moves smoothly to my side, slipping

an arm around my waist. His body is like a mountain of granite next to my wet-noodle one. I can't help but lean into him. It's either that or sit down again. He steadies my hand with the paper cup. "Take it slow," he says, and this time, I don't fight his commands. I let the warmth of him—the solidity of his body—brace me while I take a dozen small sips. My parched throat unlocks. My body starts to calm. "That's good," he says as I drain the last of the water. He takes the cup, crushes it, then tosses it to the floor. He's still holding me around the waist, but then he tips my face up to look at him. "You steady, there?"

"Fine," I mumble. I try to pull away—the closeness of him, so strong and intense, is making me uncomfortably aware of his body touching mine. My heart is racing, the fear mingling with attraction, and it's unsettling. But I'm weak, and he's not letting go.

"Hang on." He adjusts, so he's only holding my arm, not my entire body. "Can't have you breaking your head open on the slate flooring. The housekeepers would be very unhappy."

I slip him a sideways look, chastising him for the bad joke, but he's busy navigating us across the room, heading for the door. "I can walk," I say.

"Sure." He's still got a grip on me. "Otherwise, I'd carry you." He says it without a trace of a smile. I can't tell if he's joking or… if he'd actually prefer it that way.

We do this shuffle walk, him bracing me so strongly my feet barely have to carry my weight, all the way to the couches in the main room. By the time we get there, I'm feeling much better. I reach for the armrest of the couch and ease myself down into it. He lets me go this time, but it seems reluctant.

His sweeping gaze over my lightweight pajamas, loose around me as I curl up on the couch, feels hotter than it should. His dark eyes find mine. "The nightmares," he says. "Do you have them often? Or is this because of last night?" Meaning the decapitated Vardigah that almost made me throw up.

"I'm fine," I repeat. I don't want to explain that I have them every other night. That they're always the same. Except for this time with Grace. She's usually just a voice. None of that matters—it is what it is.

He's unimpressed with my answer. "Can I trust you stay put if I promise to bring you your laptop?"

That perks me right up. "You have it? How did you get here so fast—"

He holds up a finger to stop me, then points at me. "Don't move."

He waits for my agreement.

It rubs me the wrong way, but in truth, I'm still a little shaky. "Fine."

He tips his head then strides off, heading back to the bedrooms. I haven't explored the place at all, but I glimpsed other rooms further down the hall from mine. There's nothing on the couch to keep warm, but now that I've brushed off the dream, I'm not shivering so much. Ree quickly returns, and I'll be damned—he somehow got my laptop and a bag of my clothes all the way from New York. I just stare as he hands over my phone, which he must have lifted from my room and recharged. Before I can get the thanks out of my mouth, he commands me to stay put and heads off to the kitchen. I just watch him go with my mouth hanging open.

Special forces, private security, keeps his word, practically carries me to the living room after a bad dream, *and* he's making food? All while looking damn fine in a well-used pair of jeans and a black t-shirt that hugs all those muscles? And bare feet. I have a very weak spot for a man who's comfortable enough in his own skin for that. I don't think I've ever met someone as thoroughly self-contained as this man. I can't imagine anything that would make him tremble for even a second.

I blow out a low breath and place a hand flat on my closed laptop. *You're in the middle of something here, Jayda. Something really messed up. And you've got work to do. Stay focused.* But damn, this boy is hot.

Just as I'm opening my laptop, he returns with a tray filled with gorgeous food: a tiny spinach quiche, a big fluffy croissant, an enormous chocolate-dipped strawberry, and a glass of orange juice with plastic wrapped on top to keep it from spilling.

"Pain au chocolat pour madame." His accent is suddenly very French. And sexy as hell.

"I'm sorry, did you say chocolate?"

He smiles and pulls a padded chair opposite my spot on the couch. "I had *pâtisseries* brought from Paris this morning while you slept."

Is this guy for real? I decide I don't care—the food definitely is. I dive in, suddenly famished. Work can wait while I scarf this unbelievably delicious choco-late croissant.

He bites his lip while he watches me eat, his eyes darkening. I pause in my inhalation of the food. "I'm sorry, did you want some?" I say around a bite way too big to be polite.

A smile grows on his face, slowly, luxuriously,

like he's waiting for me to get the joke. Only he hasn't said anything. Finally, he says, "Yes."

I've never heard a single word filled with so much sex. I swallow my bite and set down the rest of the croissant. Then I work to clear my throat and get the heat off my face. "Help yourself." I make it clear I mean the food, not *me*. Although my body is in a full flush of heat that's screaming *me, me, me*.

"No, please." He gestures to the tray. "Continue." The smile settles into a smirk, and I feel like he hears the heat of my body more than the words coming out of my mouth.

Which is unsettling as hell. I don't understand anything that's happening here, not really, and Ree coming on to me feels wildly dangerous. Not that he would hurt me—I feel unquestionably safe. Maybe it's just his dark looks and military resumé. I force myself to remember he's part of this whole cabal of cosplayers, engaged in some insane, apparently international, game-playing that *is* dangerous— deadly so—and I want nothing to do with any of it.

I open my laptop and try to focus there. I left the office hanging with promises to get our report ready for Monday's merger meeting—I was supposed to send it to the team last night after the gallery opening. Or was that this morning? I have no idea, but my inbox is filled with people wondering where the slide deck is, and I'm still pulling the numbers together. And making up for my sketchy-as-hell attendance record lately. I tap away and quickly reassure my team that I'll have a preliminary set of numbers to them very shortly. And the slide deck after that. My fingers are flying over the keyboard, but my mouth is begging for more food, so I send off one more quick email then pause to eat again.

Ree is still studying me. "Your work is important." He says it flatly, almost like a challenge.

"Well." I take a sip of juice. *Fresh squeezed.* Oh, my God, I haven't had food this good in forever. It's always take-out or whatever I can scrounge between meetings. "It's important to *me.*" I can't claim I'm serving some higher purpose in helping one billion-dollar company scoop up another—or more often vacuum up the little guys who might be competition if they grew to full-sized before being absorbed.

Ree leans forward, his gaze intense. "And why is that?"

I chew through my strawberry, considering him a moment, but he seems genuinely curious. "I grew up in Georgia. My family wasn't poor, but they weren't exactly rich, either. Money was always tight. Life was always one blown-out tire or broken arm away from disaster, and we'd be eating out of the food pantry for a month. I determined early on I was going to do better than that. Not because I think money is everything—I work in finance; I see the guys who sell their souls for another zero in their brokerage accounts—but because I *could.* I was just as smart as anyone in my class, no matter what class, and I worked three times as hard."

"Because you had to."

It's so unexpected, it stops me cold. I have no idea how to take that.

He laces his fingers, his gaze hot on my face. "You want to prove yourself to your family."

I frown. "My family loves me, no matter what. They have my back, always. It's the rest of the world that never quite believes you're capable. I have to prove myself to the *company.* There's no room for error. No messing up. I already lost one job for a mistake that I paid for dearly… I'm not going to lose this one. And all this…" I wave around at the luxury apartment that's apparently somewhere in the French countryside. "…isn't helping. Not to mention, I just *disappeared* for two weeks—"

"You were kidnapped." His intensity ramps up.

I lean back and give him a look. "I can't tell them that!" Does he not get this at all? I set the laptop aside because I'm just too agitated—I've got to stand. I jab a finger at him. "Someone like you wouldn't understand. Everyone will look at you and just assume you know what you're doing. If something bad happened to you, well, that couldn't be *your* fault, could it? But not me. People take one look at me and assume I must have done something to *deserve* it, no matter what it was… no matter if it almost… got me killed…" I'm shaking. My finger jabbing the air is quivering, and it's fucking embarrassing.

Ree springs to his feet, so smooth and fast, I hardly realize it until he's in my face. "So you're relentless."

"What?" I pull back my hand and lean away.

"You work day and night."

"How would you know that?"

He edges closer. "You're smarter than they are. Savvier. You do all the homework. You have to understand everyone's game just to survive. And they sit back and wait for a chance to smack you down. Do you know why? Because if they had to compete on a level playing field with someone like you, they'd lose. Every time. And they know it. Trust me, they know."

I'm reeling now, just blinking and staring at him. So close. *Intense.* Like he wants to breathe me in, but instead, he's standing inches away and saying things… things I know, I've taken for granted because *of course* that's how the fucked-up world works, but he's confirming it to my face, and that rarely happens. "I can't afford to mess up."

"I know." Then he leans in, and I freeze because I think he might touch me, and I'm not sure if I want to be touched… or if I'm *dying* for him to touch me. But he just leans past me, reaching for the couch, then coming back. I'm like a statue, waiting for him to clear my space, but he hovers close and whispers, "I like a woman who knows how to get things done." Then he pulls away, and it feels like he's taking my breath with him. He's suddenly handing me my phone. "Call whoever you have to. Let me know what you need. You're not going to lose this job, Jayda. Not on my watch."

My mouth is hanging open again. He flashes a

look across my pajamas, gives me a small smirk, then swipes the juice glass off my tray and heads back to the kitchen. I watch him go, my heart thudding, and wonder what just happened. It's as if he's inside me, under my skin and in my mind. Like he knows where my secret fears live, and he just took them out, dusted them off, and tossed them aside, saying, *You got this.* I don't understand this feeling whirling inside me, but it's making me light-headed like the world is unsteady.

But in a good way, for once.

So many bad things have turned my world upside down. Why would the first good thing in a long time have to be part of all the crazy? The last time something seemed too good to be true, I let someone inside who didn't deserve it. Who wasn't what he seemed. And I can't afford that kind of hit right now—or anytime soon.

My phone buzzes in my hand.

Oh, my God, it's Grace. *Jayda, Hey! Just checking in. I have so much to tell you!*

What the hell? Just checking in? I've been sending her relentless texts since I was back in the gallery, and she's just like *Hey?* And what about the fucking Vardigah? Dread fills my chest—her hot

45

boyfriend, Theo, is part of this. And the last time I trusted the wrong person, I lost a best friend because of it, too.

I text back. *How could you do this to me?*

Ree returns with my juice refill, and the alarm on my face registers with him damn fast. "What's wrong?"

"Nothing. It's just Grace." I purse my lips and ignore his concerned attention. If all this is some massive house-of-cards lie, and that's about to become obvious, then I need to keep it cool until I can find a way out.

Grace's text comes back. *Niko says you should be safe with Ree. What's wrong??*

Some of the tension in my body drains out. I reply, *What did I tell you about answering my texts?* Because this would have been much easier if Grace had texted back even once in the last twelve hours. *And the Vardigah?? In the alley??* I add. *I've been on my own with this.* Just typing it out makes me feel better, but it also feels like a lie—especially with Ree watching me like I'm a bomb that's about to explode.

OMG I'm sorry, Grace texts back. *Be right there.*

Wait, what? *I'm in fucking France,* I start to text then Ree jerks into motion, drawing my attention—

What the hell? Grace is standing next to the couch, and Ree's got a gun trained on her. "Holy shit," I breathe.

Grace's hands belatedly go up, but Ree's already lowering his weapon and shaking his head. He points a finger at Grace. "Don't do that again."

She looks sheepish. My brain is imploding. "Did you just... *Grace.*"

"I'm sorry, I'm sorry, I'm sorry!" she gushes as she scoots around Ree to slam a hug into me. "I shouldn't have sprung the whole teleportation thing on you!" She's jabbering on about something else, hugging me hard as she kind of vibrates in place, but my body is going numb. My mind is blanking out. This isn't real. None of this is real. It can't be. Which means some time in the last twelve hours, I had a brain aneurysm or something, and all of this has been some wild-ass dream—

"Jayda?" It's Ree, his laser-focus on me even as Grace is still excessively hugging me.

She pulls back. "Oh, no. I've freaked you out."

I just blink. "I'm okay." There's a ringing in my ears.

"Oh, shit. Jayda... come sit down." Grace guides me to the couch. I'm still in my pajamas. I curl up in the corner, and it flashes me back to when our positions were reversed—Grace still recovering from her panic attack on the set, and me trying to make sure she was okay. Now she's on the couch with me, holding my hand and peering earnestly into my eyes.

I look at her hand in mine. "Tell me you're okay, Grace." That was always my anchor—get Grace through the nightmare, through the torture, and we'd all make it out the other side. She gave me a *reason* to make it through.

"I am *so good.*" She wraps her other hand around both of ours. "I know it's crazy, this whole dragon business, but it's *good.* I'm in love. I'm mated. And now I'm a dragon, too!"

That draws me out of the haze that's crowding my mind. "I'm sorry, what?"

Ree's standing behind the couch now, gripping the back, close yet not interfering, but there's fury on his face. Like he wants to tackle Grace to stop her from talking, but that invisible force field is up again.

"That's how I can teleport!" Grace's smile is crazy happy. At least in this wild dream I'm having, she seems to have found some bliss. "Theo and I are soul mates. When we made love—and holy shit, Jayda, you are not going to believe the sex!—we mated and…" She releases me and makes jazz hands. *"Magic!* Honestly, I have no idea how it works. But Theo and I are connected now in a way I can't even begin to describe. And I can shift into a dragon! And teleport! It's fucking amazing."

I'm just staring at her, mute. No idea what to say.

"Do you want me to show you my dragon?" Grace asks, eyes alight.

"No." Ree's voice is strung tight. He's going to rip holes in the couch with how hard he's gripping it. "Grace, how about we give Jayda a chance to—"

"I'm fine." I carefully unfold my legs and work my way up from the couch. One step at a time, I slowly, methodically, put distance between me and the two of them. I don't know how to escape this. How do you break out of a dream? How do you know if you've lost your mind? A deeper horror ripples through me. *Maybe I never left the torture cell.* Maybe all of the time since I've been back has been one long dream—

"Jayda." The voice is soft but masculine. *Ree.*

I've been staring at the wall. I narrow my eyes and focus on him. It seems strange that my mind would conjure someone like Ree. I've never known anyone like him. He's powerful but reserved. Strong but gentle. Sexy in a way that slips under every resistance I have. Maybe that's it—he's too perfect for me because he's not, in fact, real.

Grace scoots up next to him. "Jayda, I didn't mean to—"

"I'm fine." I feel like a robot, repeating the same lie again and again.

Grace frowns and looks hurt. Which I would care about if she were real. Real Grace would need me, not the other way around, anyway, so obviously things are even worse than I thought.

"I can take it from here," Ree says quietly to her.

"But can I just—"

"It's all right."

I turn away from them. The food is still sitting on a tray on the coffee table, but I've lost my appetite. My laptop is sitting open on the floor, tables of numbers waiting for my analysis, but that's probably part of the dream, too. My feet are the only thing that feels something, the soft squish of super-luxury carpet on my toes as I drift to the end of the couch and stare at the abstract painting on the wall. Why would my delusion bring me to France? I've never been that drawn to Europe. It's always been New York. The big apple. As far from my hometown Georgia roots as it felt I could go. And yet, I've always worked so hard that I've never had time for a play. Or the art museum. Business was where my head was always at.

None of this makes sense.

FOUR

Ree

I finally convince Grace to teleport back to wherever she came from.

Fuck, Jayda's a mess. She's staring at the abstract painting I purchased from a Parisian art gallery fifty years ago. I've long ago forgotten the artist. She's examining its broad swirls like they hold the secret to coming out of whatever fugue has gripped her.

"Grace has left," I say.

She doesn't respond.

"She teleported back to her dragon soul mate." Maybe I can jolt her out of this. Every muscle in my body tenses, willing her to shake it off.

Jayda slowly turns her head to me. "You're trying to annoy me."

"Is it working?" I give her half a smile.

She frowns. "This isn't a game."

"Isn't it?" I prod. "What did you call it? A *fucking cosplay gang war,* I believe."

The frown grows darker. She turns to face me fully. "None of this is real."

"You'd better hope it is."

She grits her teeth. Her fists curl up.

That's right, fight it, mon trésor. "Because if none of this is real, then you're not safe at all. And nothing I can do can protect you."

Her eyes widen a little, the fear claiming them, and it runs a chill through my heart. But I need her to accept the unacceptable, not shut it out or shut down or whatever trick her mind is playing on her to reject what her eyes have seen plain before her.

"I'm a dragon." I hold her gaze so she can't look away. "And a man. I've lived for two hundred and ten years as such, and I can tell you, most humans are weak. They cannot endure the things you have. They can't accept things they don't understand. But you're not like them. You're dragon spirited. It's why you were taken by the Vardigah. It's why they tried to destroy you. But there's too much fire in you to be put out by the likes of them. You're too strong."

"I'm not." It's a whisper. Her lips tremble with it.

53

God, I want to take her in my arms. But she's not there yet. "Don't lie to me."

"It's true!" Her eyes are glassing with tears, but they're angry. Her fists rise, and she shakes them in front of her. "I can't do this… this is *crazy…*"

I grip her shoulders. "It's real. Accept it."

"No!" She slams her fists into my chest.

It loosens my hold, so I release her.

She cradles one hand like it hurts. *"Goddamnit,"* she mutters. But it sounds clearer.

"Am I a little too real for you?" I tease.

"You're really fucking annoying!" she snaps.

The tension in my body eases. "Hit me again," I say.

"You're a SEAL or some shit," she snarls. "I'm not going to fight you."

"I didn't say *fight*. I said *hit me.*" I put up my hands, palms flat to her, like sparring mitts. "You look like a woman who knows how to throw a punch. Aim for the center of my palm." I've seen her work out at the kickboxing gym she likes to frequent. I know this is how she vents all that time at the office, dealing with the assholes of the financial world.

She's glaring at me, but then she growls and winds up to throw the punch. I catch it, gently, letting my hand give just enough resistance, so it's not like she's slamming her beautiful hand into a rock. I want those hands on me, someday—they need to not be broken.

She's breathing hard now, but not like before—this is controlled. Angry, but real. She throws a punch at the other hand. I catch it, softly, open-handed, then ease off.

"That's it," I say. "But harder. Hit me like I'm the fucking Vardigah."

She sets her teeth and punches again. One-two. Right-left. I step back, so she has further to reach, but she comes closer again. One-two. Growling with each throw. *Fuck me,* this is turning me on, and that is *not* my intent.

"Harder," I say through my teeth.

She groans in frustration and punches again. One-two. One-two. But they're cleaner shots with more power. Her hair is wild around her face. Her knuckles are reddening with the impact. I can go like this all day—that's a lie; I wouldn't be able to keep my hands off her—but she needs to vent this and be done.

"Come on, now," I goad her. "They fucking tortured you. They're real, they're bastards, and they took everything from you. If they were standing here right now, you would *not* play patty cake. Put all your anger into it. Give me all of it."

She growl-groans again and pummels me, a flurry of punches that has me stepping back because she's leaning in so hard. Then there's something under my foot—her laptop?—and I'm off-kilter just as she screams out her rage and whirls and catches me with a full-on, spinning back kick. It knocks me square in the chest, and I'm afraid I'll wipe out her computer, so I take the fall.

Somehow, I forget the coffee table and manage to smash it to pieces on the way down.

"Oh, *shit.*" Jayda's hands un-fist and fly to her mouth. Then she leaps forward and kneels down. "Oh my God, Ree! Are you okay?" Her hands are on me—just light on my chest, but I reflexively reach up, both hands in her hair, cupping her cheeks as she looms over me. She's freaked and concerned, but it's all about me, which is perfect. She freezes at my touch, lips parted, breathing hard.

I'm aching to pull her down into a kiss. "Does that feel real to you?"

She doesn't move away. "Yes," she breathes. Then she shivers and pulls out of my hold, rocking back on her knees, then standing up and peering down at me. Her eyes are still dilated. I know it affects her. "You okay?"

I smirk. "You don't have to worry about me."

She steps back, and it's a little unsteady. As I'm picking myself up out of the coffee table debris field —complete with destroyed breakfast and splattered orange juice that will be a nightmare to clean— Jayda turns and stumbles toward the kitchen. I brush myself off and follow. The kitchen is good sized with a center island and professional appliances, for when I'm in the mood to cook, but she's just after a glass of water, which she's chugging as I enter. She sets the glass down and braces her hands against the counter, breathing heavily.

Everything about her is enticing, from her cloud of silky curls to her bare feet on the floor. Her pajamas are loose and rumpled. Her pulse has to be elevated already. She's pumped from the fight, the fall, and now whatever conclusion she's coming to about all of this.

And I want to cement in her mind the *reality* of this situation.

I ease up behind her, one hand skimming her waist, the other threading up into her hair from below. She sighs like she expects it—she doesn't pull away, but she's not melting into my touch, either.

"I don't need a man."

I massage her scalp a little, nudging her head to the side so I can brush her ear with my lips. "Didn't say you did," I whisper along her skin. I feel the shudder that runs through her.

"But if I did, I'd want a grown-ass man. Not someone who plays dress-up."

I nuzzle her neck. "I'm a grown man." My cock is hard enough for her to feel, but she's still resisting, still holding away from my body. I slide my hand across the top of her pajamas, my palm flat against her belly, my fingers dipping below the waistband. "I'm very good at precisely two things," I whisper against her neck, dying for the first taste. "Killing anything that would hurt you and knowing how to make you come." She sucks in a breath as I pull her back against me, the hardness of my cock pressing into the softness of her rear. "Tell me to stop," I say as I slide my hand down between her legs. The downy softness of her mound, the slick wetness below. She's pulling air between her teeth now, arms rigid as she presses her hands into the counter. I dip a finger into her folds, stroking slow and steady, while my other hand is fisting and pulling her hair, slowly bending her head back, bringing her more strongly against me, so I can have full access to pleasure her body. My cheek is pressed to hers. Both of us are breathing hard now. "Tell me you want this." I stroke her nub. She squirms against me. "Tell me you *need* this." She lets go of the counter with one hand and grabs at my arm, the one halfway down her pants, but it's not to stop me. I use my teeth to rake across her cheek. *"Say it."*

She shudders in my arms. "I need this."

Fuck yes. I let go of her hair and wrap my arm around her chest, the heavy globe of her breast full in my hand as I pull her hard against me. She arches up, on her toes, legs spread as she leans back into me, giving me more access, and I use it all. My hand works that sweet, hot wetness, thrumming her nub, stroking her long and hard, thrusting *up* and inside with two fingers and then three. I'm working her hard, and she's squirming and moaning, racing there so fast, she must have needed it bad.

"Oh, yes," I breathe, the jostle of her body against my cock exquisite.

She's pushing against the counter, against me, jolting as I stroke her, but she's hardly making a sound. Only a humming sort of whimper that's climbing higher and higher. Then she gasps and convulses, both the shudder of her sex and the shaking of her body. She cries out, "Fuck!" just once, and then a soft moaning whimper as she comes down the other side. Slowly, she melts into me, the pleasure making her soft and pliable, a goddess in repose against my body.

Oh, the things I want to do with her.

I pull my hand from between her legs and turn her around to face me. Her eyes are beautifully lidded, nearly closed in her post-orgasmic haze. She leans back against the counter, her hands lazy against my shoulders.

"Holy shit, Ree," she breathes. She fumbles for my cock like she thinks she'll return the favor.

Not even close.

I lean in fast, pressing my body against hers and burrowing my face into her hair. "Did that feel real?"

She laughs a little, in a breathy way. Then her breath hitches as I pull her slightly away from the counter. I slide my hands down the gorgeous round of her bottom, taking her pajamas and letting them fall once they're past her thighs.

"Oh," she says, then, "I have protection."

"That's nice." I grab her under the arms and hoist her up on the counter.

She makes a noise of surprise, and her eyes fly open. Then I don't see her expression as I bury my face between her legs, but I hear the gasp of surprise, the clutch of her hand against my shoulder. I fling away the pajama bottoms and continue my feast on her blossoming sex, hooking her legs over my shoulders and holding her fast in place.

"Oh God." I hear her bang into the cupboard as she arches back. "Ree... *yes,"* follows as I add my fingers to the mix, thrusting hard as I flick my tongue in a way that has her gasping and squirming. "Fuck, yes, God, just like that, oh please, Ree, God, *please."* Her babbling is an elixir. I lap at her and thrust and work for every word, every gasp, every exclamation as she builds to a climax that has her shrieking and shaking and digging her fingers into my shoulder. I keep going until every tremor has worked loose. Then I ease up the torment, come up for air, and wipe my face clear of the sopping wetness that's literally making the floor slick.

"Jesus, Ree," she says as I boost her down from the counter.

She makes a play for my cock once again, but I catch her wrist and give it an open-mouthed kiss. "I'll take care of that."

"What?" She's dazed. Beautifully dazed by pleasure.

I kiss her softly on the cheek and nuzzle her a little. Then I pull back to look her in the eyes. I can't keep the smirk off my face. I've left her so sated she's not sure what to do next.

"Take a shower," I say. "Get dressed. Then come work on whatever you need for that big meeting tomorrow." I step back. My erection is ridiculously prominent, bulging out from my jeans. I ignore that, simply take her hand in mine, scoop her pajamas off the floor, and lead her half-naked out of the kitchen. In any other situation, I'd be taking her to my bedroom for some serious, extended play, but she has work to do, and I meant what I said about that. She won't be losing her dreams and ambitions because of the dragon world, and certainly not because of the Vardigah, not on my watch.

When we reach the door of her room, I kiss her lightly on the cheek again, give her the pajama bottoms, and wave her off to the shower. She stumbles in that direction, still a little orgasm-drunk, and I grin all the way to my room. I've already set up the camera feed, piping it straight into my bathroom, where I can see it from the open shower. I brace against the wall and stroke my way to bliss as

I watch Jayda drop the rest of her pajamas and climb into her own shower.

She takes her time soaping and rinsing, long and luxurious, *bless her.*

I come twice more before I'm done.

FIVE

Jayda

I DON'T NEED A MAN TO COMPLETE ME.

But *damn* Ree is a man I'd like to fill me up.

I'm putting the finishing touches on my presentation for the merger meeting, which is in less than an hour, but I keep getting distracted. Not by Ree—he's been nothing but professional since yesterday's hot kitchen orgasms. He cleared out the destroyed coffee table and brought in a new one, then he stayed out of my way while I worked. He brought me tea and then dinner, then insisted I turn in at a reasonable time to fight the jet lag, and that I could finish the rest the next morning. Because just before 2pm French time today, we will be teleporting into the 8am merger meeting in New York.

Insane.

But I've accepted that, whatever else might be going on, the teleportation is real. Grace really did pop in to France to visit me—she apparently can because she's a "mated dragon," the details of which I'm not sure I want to know. Niko returned to Ree's apartment—which is really a fucking *castle* —and we practiced teleporting all over the grounds just so I'd be used to it before the meeting. I have no idea if Ree is royalty on top of his elite private security employment, but one thing is certain—I've never had a man take care of me so thoroughly. And competently. Before I can even think about having breakfast, it's there. He arranges for a printer to be delivered to the apartment before I realize I need one. Even the clothes he retrieved from my apartment in New York are perfect for the presentation… with one exception.

The shoes. Genuine Prada, Italian Saffiano leather, black stiletto. I was wearing them when the Vardigah grabbed me right out of my apartment. I carefully parked them in one corner of my cell, a promise that someday, I would get back to *normal* again. Only when I did, I couldn't stand to put them on. But they were $700 shoes! I couldn't just throw them away. And somehow Ree found them, paired them with my best suit, and brought the whole thing back so I would be properly dressed for the presentation.

I don't have the heart to say anything about it.

Ree steps out from the kitchen where he's been cleaning up lunch, phone in hand. "Niko says he's ready when you are."

I close my laptop. "I'm ready."

He nods and quickly texts something. A moment later, Niko teleports into the great room of Ree's apartment-within-a-castle. I slip on my shoes, slide the laptop into my carry case with my notes and the handouts for the board, and straighten my suit when I stand.

"All set?" Niko's dressed casually, jeans and a t-shirt, but he's just getting us to New York, not walking us into the building.

I nod.

When I wasn't paying attention, Ree changed into all black—suit, tie, black dress shirt. He looks *exactly* like a high-end bodyguard, which is what his cover story will be. Only it's not really a cover story at all—he's not letting me out of his sight, outside of the apartment, because we still don't know how the Vardigah found Grace in that alley by the gallery.

"Any word on the Vardigah?" Ree asks Niko as

we line up for transport. Niko will hold Ree's shoulder. Ree will hold my hand. I'll carry the laptop case.

Niko grimaces. "They ransacked Grace's apartment."

"What?" I stop fussing with my case and snap my attention to him.

"She wasn't there," he adds quickly. "We don't know what they were looking for or how they found the place. We're looking for the connection between the alley outside the gallery and Grace's apartment."

"Other than Grace?" I lift an eyebrow.

"Except Grace wasn't home when it happened." Niko shakes his head. "And we still don't think they can track people, just *places*. It doesn't make sense. But we'll figure it out. In the meantime," he says to Ree, "don't let her out of your sight."

"Copy that." Ree's calm tone belies the hard grip he has on my hand.

"I don't like this trip to the city," Niko says to me. "Are you sure this is necessary?"

"It is," Ree backs me up.

Which I appreciate, but I can speak for myself. "It won't take long. An hour tops. Then I can work remotely for a while."

"Good." Niko grasps hold of Ree's shoulder, and an instant later, we're at the back of an alley a block away from the building where *Supreme Acquisitions and Holdings* has their headquarters on Wall Street. Normally, I work in a satellite office in Midtown, but the merger meetings are almost always at corporate. "All right," Niko says. "Text me when you need transport back." Then he disappears.

Ree adjusts the sleeve of his jacket while scouring the area around us.

"I doubt the Vardigah are hiding behind the dumpster," I say. We haven't spoken much since yesterday, beyond the normal back-and-forth necessary to get ready for today. Ree's made no move to repeat the sizzling hot sex we had the day before. Or should I say, the sizzling hot orgasms *he gave me.* I'm still wondering when I get to pay him back for that. This is the first I've come close to teasing him.

He gives me a tight smile. "Situational awareness." He moves me down the alley toward the street. "I have a feeling our exposure is worse tucked away here. I want to get you into a crowd."

My heels click down the pavement in rapid succession as we hurry toward the street. Once there, it's packed, people striding to their morning meetings or filling taxis on their way through the financial district. Ree stays close, his hand on my elbow, navigating the crowd with me. We quickly reach the building, and Ree has plenty of credentials to get through security, but I vouch for him as my personal bodyguard. We stride to the elevators and ride up.

"I'll be in the room with you," he says, casually, hands clasped in front of his black suit. "Just pretend I'm not there. Do your thing."

I smirk. "You're not an easy man to ignore, Ree."

He slides me a look that's hot as sin. "Later," he says, then looks forward again, all business.

My body temperature rises at least a degree with that promise. I struggle full-time for the rest of the elevator ride to get re-focused on business again. Everyone's gotten their board packets. I've reviewed the numbers with the team. They've agreed with my recommendations. It's just a matter of selling it to the board—or at least convincing them I've done the proper due diligence behind the merger, whatever they decide. The elevator arrives, I lead the way out, and Ree slips behind to follow just like he's my assistant or groupie or something. The receptionist for the company does a double-take—*yes, girl, he is just that fine*—but then slides us both guest badges. The conference room is mid-sized. Ostentatious enough to feel right for these high-profile business meetings, but practical enough to not feel like we're lost in a coliseum.

Ten board members, my three team members from *Supreme,* and the CEO of the buyer corporation. The buyer and seller will meet later to negotiate terms. This meeting is to brief the buyer and make the recommendation for acquisition. *Supreme* will help with negotiations, although Anthony will take the lead on that part. And once a deal has been struck, *Supreme* will again step in to help guide the Project Team on the acquisition process itself. That's Jim and Arnie's expertise. I'm the numbers lady—the one who brings the data and the charts and runs the calculations to say whether this deal is a win for the buyer or not. It's not the highest-profile position on the team, but everyone knows that getting it right is critical.

I briefly introduce Ree as my personal security, relaying a suitably distressing story about how I received threatening notes, and then my apartment was broken into. Fictitious for me, but Ree said it actually happened to one of his clients. That gives a weird vibe to the introductions, but Ree's already faded into the background of the conference room, as promised, and once I get through the glad-handing and set up my laptop, I really do forget for the next half hour that he's there. I have everyone's attention, and this is my moment to show them what I've got. Numbers and charts, sure, but also the depth of research that *Supreme*—and me in particular—have brought to the room. I need to sell them on my expertise as well as the deal they're considering. Which I finish off with my recommendation to buy, then field questions for another half hour. It takes time, but there's nothing I don't have an answer for. Anthony's giving me encouraging looks, and Jim's not jumping in like he usually does, trying to explain my charts for me. Even Arnie seems to think the work is acceptable, even if he still stares at my boobs the entire time. At least he's not tossing up his usual backhanded compliment about how it was remarkable I could get all this done with having only been with the company less than six months—conveniently ignoring my MBA and seven years of experience prior to *Supreme*. Maybe even he realizes that shit has no place here. We're conducting serious business—it's all about the numbers, and I have the receipts.

When we wrap up, there's more handshaking,

and the board has yet to vote, but I can read the room—they will move forward with the deal. Based on the strength of my presentation. I'm floating on the smiles of my team, my steps light in my designer shoes as Ree and I retrace our steps back out of the office and to the elevator. I decide he was right to bring the shoes. He was right about getting that extra sleep. And he basically made this whole thing possible while still keeping me safe. I'm feeling gushes of gratitude that I'd like to *physically* express in the near future.

I keep it professional until we're in the elevator alone.

Then I tip my head back, raise my arms, and shout, "Yes!"

Ree smirks at me from where he stands by the elevator buttons. "If I ever need to acquire a $500M dollar company, I know who to call."

I drop my arms, do a fist pump, then smooth out my suit jacket because we're almost to the ground floor. "And I'll take good care of you, Mr. Cendrillion." I smirk as the elevator door opens, letting that double entendre just hang there until we get back to France. Which is crazy, and I really should find out more about this whole dragon business, including this ability to teleport, but to be honest, I mostly want to mount Ree's hard-ass body and ride him until I can't see.

Ree's at my side, going ahead of me through the revolving door. The street traffic is a little less, but Ree's large, black-suit-clad body still clears a path. He pulls out his phone just as we reach the alley, which he sweeps with his scrutinizing gaze before focusing on the phone briefly to text Niko. I'm still feeling light as a feather, floating on the accomplishment of the meeting.

My own phone buzzes, and it's Anthony. *You nailed it. Vote 10-0 to proceed. Congrats.* I turn to tell Ree, but suddenly, the alley is *filled* with people.

Holy shit—

Vardigah. Those pointy-eared bastards teleported into the alley! And a half dozen of them surround Ree. He pulls a gun from inside his jacket and shoots two in rapid succession. But another four surround *me.* Just as they close in, Niko appears out of nowhere, right between me and the closest Vardigah. Then Niko disappears, and a massive black dragon appears in his place! The surprise of it knocks me back, my bag goes flying and my ankle twists, breaking one of the heels of those damn shoes. I collide with the brick wall of the alley, and the broken shoe comes off completely, but I manage to stay upright. Niko's dragon lashes out at one Vardigah with his tail while slashing at the other with razor-sharp, six-inch fangs. I can't even see Ree down the alley, but one of the Vardigah slips past Niko's massive black-scaled body and comes after me. I reach down and wrench off the remaining shoe that still has a stiletto heel and throw it with all my might. Miraculously, it stabs the Vardigah straight through the eye—the bastard reels back in shock, then collapses. Niko's dragon disappears, and now he's standing naked in the alley. *What?* Before I can think twice about that, he lurches over the Vardigah body parts he's left behind and grabs my arm. An instant later, we're back in the great room of Ree's apartment.

"Where's Ree?" I screech at Niko, but he's already gone.

I stand there, in the silent room, for ten heart-stopping seconds.

Suddenly, Niko reappears with Ree, both naked —*only Ree is covered in blood.*

"Oh, my God!" I lurch forward.

Niko's bracing him. "You okay?" he asks Ree. Niko has somehow rescued my bag, which he sets down on the floor.

Ree gives a curt nod, but he's breathing hard. "What the *fuck*, Niko."

"I know," Niko says. "I don't see how they found her."

Ree's got fury on his face, but all I see is the blood. "She's not going back to New York," he says to Niko. "Go on, take care of it. Then *call me.*" He waves Niko off.

Niko looks briefly at me—I'm frantic but unharmed—then disappears.

"Ree." I don't know where I can even touch him. There's blood splashed across his chest and running down his arm.

"I'm okay."

But he's not.

SIX

Ree

GODDAMNIT. The fucking Vardigah came back—
and in force.

The adrenaline of the fight masked, for the critical seconds of the battle, my utter terror that they'd
found Jayda. But it was fucking *glorious* to slice those
bastards to pieces, after all they've done, and not
just to Jayda and the other women—I've waited two
hundred years for that payback. But now we're back
in France, and all I can do is pray they can't track
her here. We got lucky in the alley. Niko had mated-
dragon strength, and I've literally trained my entire
life to take down bad guys when they launch a
surprise attack. But the Vardigah were prepared this
time—they came in numbers. If they find us here in
the south of France, it'll be just me against who

knows how many of them. Under no circumstances can I let Jayda out of my sight.

"Jesus, you're *bleeding*, Ree!" She's standing in front of me, barefoot but unharmed, her hands fluttering like she wants to do something.

I'm naked and covered in blood. My arm throbs where one of them got me. I wipe the blood from my shoulder to get a better look. "One of them had a vibrating sword of some kind." There's a deep gash that's making my arm useless. I clamp my hand over it to stem the bleeding.

"You need to go to the hospital!" She's spooling up.

"I'll be fine," I tell her, but the panic in her eyes says she doesn't believe me.

"I'll get some towels." She spins to go, but I grab her wrist. *"You need help!"* she protests.

I pull her closer. "You're not leaving my sight. Understood?"

She nods, but she's tearing up. It's a stress reaction, I know that—I've got an insane amount of adrenaline still pumping through me—but I need to calm her down and get myself patched up. And I know she doesn't understand how dragon healing works and how this isn't much. I'll be fine soon.

"You can help me get cleaned up, okay?" I slide

my good hand—bloody and fucking disgusting, but at least functional—down to hold hers. She doesn't shy away from it. I walk us both back toward the bedrooms, skipping hers and heading straight for mine. Probably trailing blood across the carpet, but that can't be helped. When we reach the bathroom, I grab a hand towel and press it to my shoulder. "Come here and hold this for me, okay?" That brings her closer—I've got this insane need to be touching her at all times, like that will somehow ward off the Vardigah—and she does a great job of putting pressure on my wound. Fucking *hurts,* but not for long. I lean back against the counter and slide my hand around her waist, drawing her and her gorgeous suit up against my naked and bloody body. She doesn't even hesitate, just leans in and alternates worried looks between the rapidly-soaking towel and my face, which is probably also a mess. Somewhere on me, I have Vardigah blood as well. I'm a complete disaster.

She's distressed. "I need you to not bleed out on me, Ree." She's trying to sound stern, but I hear the panic underneath it. "Who's going to protect me if you're passed out on the floor?"

"No one's passing out." It feels good to have her this close. *Reassuring.* There's part of this attack that's shaken something loose inside me. "Dragons have ridiculous healing powers—it's part of the magic. I was born in 1810, Jayda. You don't live as long as I have, especially not in the work I do, without having something a little supernatural to keep you going."

Her expression is still pinched, but I can feel her body relaxing against me. The closeness has to be affecting her, too. "Don't tell me nothing can kill you."

"No, we definitely can be killed." I give her a small smile. I can already feel my shoulder knitting itself together under the constant pressure she's putting on the towel. "But you have to really fuck us up to accomplish it. Or cut off our heads. Or simply wait long enough. Unmated dragons will wither away after a couple hundred years. We can die of a broken heart, as it were."

She scowls and looks away from my close and probably too-intense gaze. "What the hell is this *mated* business? Grace said she was a mated dragon now, and I just…" She purses her lips. "It's still too crazy to believe."

"Did you believe the bloodbath in the alley?" I tease.

She growls and presses harder on my towel.

I pretend to wince, even though it's mostly healed now.

"Okay, *fine*. The magic is real. *Really messed up*, if you ask me." Then she stops talking and seems to consider her words for a moment. "Thank you." She meets my gaze. "You've been really good to me. And you saved my life. I just…" She's opening her heart to me, and that's more terrifying to me than a dozen Vardigah coming at me with swords.

"Now you owe me a gratitude fuck, right?" I joke. It's forced. My heart spasms a little, and it's not from the blood loss.

"Well, not anymore." She scowls. The hurt on her face stabs me right through that wobbly heart I've suddenly got.

"Good." I peel her hand off my shoulder and use the towel to wipe away the blood. There's a bright pink scar running from the meat of my shoulder down nearly to my elbow. "See? Good as new." It'll still ache for another hour, then it actually *will* be as if I were never injured. Eventually, even the scar will fade.

She marvels at it, leaning away from me. "How is that possible?"

I toss the towel in the sink. "Perks of being a dragon." Since the hand on my injured side isn't useless anymore, I put it to work—unbuttoning Jayda's suit jacket.

Her eyes go wide… but she's not stopping me.

"I don't need your gratitude," I say, sliding the jacket off her shoulders and letting it fall to the floor. "But dragons are horny as fuck." I start on her blouse and lean in closer, letting the nearness of my body and my growing hard-on speak for themselves. "Especially after a fight," I whisper against her neck. "Or a shift. Or being near incredibly sexy women with brains that give me hard-ons for days."

She sucks in a breath as I open her blouse and let it fall off her shoulders, following the jacket to the floor. Her breasts are high and full, and my cock stiffens the rest of the way, ready for her. I drop an open-mouthed kiss on her neck, tasting and filling up on the exquisite smell of *her*, while I slip a finger under her bra strap and slide it off her shoulder.

"Ree." The *need* in her voice just amps up mine. "Are you sure you're okay?"

"No." I pull back and lick my lips, tasting her on them. "I need your help with something." I take her hands in mine and turn, so I'm pulling her as I step backward toward my walk-in shower.

Her eyelids flutter. "What's that?"

I lift one of her hands and lace my fingers with

it, urging her into the shower with me. There's no door—it's one of those open rainfall types activated by a touchless sensor on the wall. I wave my hand to start it up. The water falls in a square column behind me. I bring her to the edge of it with me and grab the soap off the tiny inset shelf in the rock wall.

I hand it to her. "Wash me." Everything in me tightens in anticipation of her hands all over me.

Her lips part and her eyes dilate. I step enough into the stream that it slides a small cascade down my face and over my shoulders, washing away some of the blood and gore. She steps closer, right up against me, then reaches behind me to get the bar of soap wet. With a look that has me aching, she lathers up the soap in front of my face, sets the bar aside, and starts running those dark, beautiful hands all over my body.

Fuck. Me.

I hold absolutely still. My cock is a rod that she brushes with her skirt, which is slowly getting soaked while her hands soap up every inch of my chest. She gets more soap and covers my belly, methodically getting every dip and curve of muscle, meticulously moving on to my thighs and down to my calves, kneeling before me, her springy curls getting wet from the spray. She's assiduously avoiding my aching cock. Then she looks up from where she's crouched, giving me a saucy look.

"I think you missed a spot," I say through gritted teeth.

She smirks then slowly runs her hands up the inside of my legs. When she reaches my balls, I can't help the intake of breath, but she lavishes a *hell* of a lot of time on them, ignoring my cock trapped between us now. Her soaked-through bra clings to her skin, giving me an early peek at the glory of her nipples, dark and dusky, underneath.

"Did I miss something?" Her smile is fully at my expense.

"Are you quite done?" Even I can hear the strain in my voice.

"Not quite." Then she grabs my cock and strokes it hard.

"Fuck!" escapes me before I can stop it. I'm done messing around. I grab her around the waist and pull her into the downpour. The soap is gone in an instant, and we're both blinded by the spray. By feel alone, I reach behind her and unhook her bra, casting that aside under the shower. Then I bring those gorgeous breasts against my chest as I reach behind to unzip her skirt and send that to the floor.

Her panties are all that's left, but I'm saving those. I turn her, my cock now rubbing against her rear as I cup her breasts from behind, finding those luscious nipples, already hard before my fingers twist them. She gasps, and the full-body-press of hers against mine is driving me mad. I wrap one arm around her waist, so I've got her securely, and half-carry, half-walk her to the edge of the shower. We're sopping wet, but now we can see. The spray is still warm on my back and trickling over her body. I slide down her panties, then find her hands and place them on the wall. She has to lean slightly forward to manage it, which leaves her in the perfect position for me. I reach for the small, hidden drawer in the wall that holds the condoms and bring one out.

She twists to see what I'm doing.

I rip the package with my teeth and sheath myself with her watching. "Now's the time to tell me if you don't want my cock."

The look on her face says anything but. "And if I don't tell you?"

I slide behind her again, my hand braced against the wall by hers, my cock in position. I glide my hand across her hip, enjoying the roundness of her bottom before I take her. "You're going to find out just how horny a dragon can be." I thrust hard, taking her all the way, burying myself to the hilt. *"Fuck,"* I gasp. She's *so* tight.

"Oh, God." She's clawing at the wall. *"Ree."*

"Yes?" I pull out and thrust in again. I'm just getting acquainted. The feel of her clenching me. The slickness of her skin. The incredible heat of her sex.

Her one hand leaves the wall and reaches back, grasping at my leg, urging me on.

I grab hold of both her hips and thrust hard.

"Shit!" she cries out, bracing with both hands against the wall again.

"You better hold onto that wall," I warn her. Because this holding back will not work for me. I pull out almost all the way and thrust in again, garnering a whimper from her. I do it harder, and that fucking sexy noise is louder. Then I pound, thrust after thrust into the hotness of her sex. The aching tension deep in my balls coils tighter. *"Fuck. Yes."* I'm gasping with how good she feels, how right, how sweet each thrust is, piling one on top of another and rocketing me up.

"Ree. Oh, my God, Ree!" She's getting there fast, too.

I lean in, pushing her closer to the wall, bracing

my hand against it and changing my angle, so I'm thrusting more *up* and taking us both higher.

"Oh, fuck, please, please," she's begging me. And while I'd love to ride out her orgasm and give her another, I'm almost there already. I reach my hand around to that hot little nub she has, all the while thrusting like a madman, lifting her up on her toes with the force of it. I work her sweet spot as I pick up the pace, and she cries out, shaking and shivering and clenching all around my cock. That tips me right over, and suddenly, I'm shooting inside her. I keep thrusting through it, but I'm blind with pleasure. It's blowing my mind, whiting everything out, so intense, I can barely breathe. I'm wildly thrusting through the rest of it, panting and drawing it out, not wanting it to end, but of course it does. Slowly. With a spreading buzz through my entire body. I can barely tell where mine ends and hers begins, we're so welded together, up against the rock wall of my shower, breathing heavily through our still-tingling orgasms. It lingers like I've seldom felt before, the aftershocks still coming, making me twitch inside her. She's doing the same, softly swearing and shuddering against me.

I finally stop the slow wind-down of thrusting and simply hold her. "Holy *fuck*, Jayda," I whisper against her shoulder. "Do you have any idea… how good that was…" My mind is a scramble. I legit feel like I can't move, or I might shatter.

"Is this the magic?" she asks, her voice half laugh, half wonder. "I can't feel my toes."

I laugh lightly. I can't remember the last time I did that. I hold her tighter against me, my cock still buried deep inside her. "Oh, *God*, the things I want to do to you."

"I thought you just did them." It's like she doesn't think there's more.

There's so much more. "Baby, I'm just getting started." And like that, I can feel my cock stiffening again. I move slightly, making a promise of more to come, and the way she moans against the wall feels like I've found a secret nirvana.

I knew it would be good with her.

I had no fucking clue.

I'm so completely, utterly lost.

SEVEN

Jayda

REE IS KISSING ME EVERYWHERE—*EVERYWHERE*—BUT on my mouth.

I've never had so much sex in a single day. If the teleportation and dragon-shifting and miraculous healing hadn't convinced me that magic truly was real, the unearthly sexual stamina would have. I've been with all kinds of men—Ree's cock is *not* of this world. Not in size, not in girth, not in the time to be fuck-ready after orgasm. He's a certifiable sex miracle.

That doesn't even count his lovemaking skills, which are also unreal.

I called a halt to it earlier in the evening. I'm only human. I had to shower, eat, check my fucking email… but now that the office has stopped barraging me with follow-ups to the morning meeting, Ree's back, feasting on me. I'm sitting at the kitchen table, laptop finally closed, and he's come up behind me to entice me back into his sexual wonderland. He's gathered up my hair in a bunch so he can move my head just where he wants me. Right now, that's tilted to the side so he can consume my neck, one nipping kiss after another, down to my shoulder. He slides my blouse and bra strap down, slipping his hand down to free my breast. He manhandles that while running his tongue across my collarbone, then back up along my jawbone, ending at my ear, which he bites in a way that sends sparks between my legs. Then he switches sides, consuming every inch of my skin, whatever he can reach from the back of the chair, without me moving a muscle. He wants me to just allow it. Relax and let him squeeze my breasts, massage my scalp, feast upon the back of my neck, my cheeks, even my eyelids after he's brushed them closed.

I've never felt so *desired* by a man.

It's a thing completely separate from the fucking. And *Oh Lordy* do we fuck. That heavenly cock

ALISA WOODS

and my abused lady parts have been in so much intimate contact, I thought for sure I'd be crazy sore by now. But then Ree would go down on me and lavish his attention there. Something about dragon saliva having healing properties. I don't know about that, but his *tongue* brings me a little closer to heaven. Then somehow, I'm able to take that enormous cock once more. I'm sure that's on the menu soon, after he consumes my upper body as an *hors d'oeuvre*, but right now, Ree's attentions are all about worshipping my shoulders and neck, and when I make the slightest attempt to reach for him, he holds my wrists far apart until I promise not to touch.

But I can still talk. "You're pretty hot for two hundred and ten."

I feel the huff of his laugh against my skin.

"How many women have you had in all those years?"

He pauses for just a half-second, then he straightens up and turns my chair around to face him. My blouse and bra are around my waist, baring my breasts.

"None half as amazing as you." He kneels between my legs, spreading them wide so he can lean in and tease my tight nipples with his tongue.

I play with his hair, which must not violate the "no touch" rule because he allows it. "You don't have to flatter me, Ree. I'm already your sex toy."

He freezes again, then he bites me, so tender, yet it's electric. He peers up as he kisses over the bite marks. "You're no toy. And I don't flatter."

I believe him about that. I've never met someone as straight as Ree has been with me, even from the first moment. I trail my fingers across his cheek, just a gentle caress, but he pulls away from it. Then he manhandles my breast again, lifting the nipple so he can flick at it with his tongue. I let my fingers retreat to threading through his hair again. That seems safe.

"So, you've never mated, then."

He freezes. My heart stutters. *Did I just offend him?* He looks up, still holding my breast, peering into my eyes. "No." I don't even understand this mating business, but if Theo and Grace are already hooked up, I don't understand why Ree wouldn't be. Then he stands suddenly and moves behind my chair again. I'm afraid I've said something awful without realizing it, but he returns a moment later… with a condom in his hand. He takes my hand and tugs me up from the chair. Then he pulls me against him, my upper half naked against his t-shirt, his erection strong against my belly. He's in casual track pants, and I'm only wearing yoga pants, so I can feel every bit of his length.

"I need you," he says roughly. "Right now." He walks me two steps back, up against the kitchen table. He slides his hands down my backside, baring my bottom, then hoists me up on the surface. Then he quickly pulls down his own pants, rolls on the condom, and before I can say anything, he's thrusting fast inside me.

"Oh," is all I get out before he gets serious about fucking. His hands hard on my bottom, holding me in place, him thrusting hard into me, grunting as he does. Every time we do this, I can't believe how huge he is—like each time, my body is all *holy shit you're getting laid,* and it just quivers and tries to take in all his glory. I nearly always come right away, as if it's a shock orgasm. *Sweet mercy, we are getting fucked, hallelujah.* This time is no different. Ree is pounding into me, grunting and groaning and bottoming out, his fingers digging deep into my ass as my heels bang on his legs. My arms wrap around his neck, holding on for dear life. The orgasm starts deep inside, where his cock strokes me hard, and trembles like an earthquake, building then suddenly letting loose. I'm cursing and shaking and arching

into his glorious body. I take a moment to come back from that. Ree's breathing hard, but he's barely worked up. I know what that means—we're visiting at least two more positions before he'll let himself come.

Sure enough, he pulls out and turns me over. I'm now bent in half, sprawled across the table, and he takes me immediately from behind, thrusting so hard, we're jittering the table on the smooth tiles of the kitchen and banging the wall. *God, he's big*—and he fills me so deep in this position. He loves it, too. I can tell by the grunts with each thrust, the way he digs his fingers into my backside, and how he runs his hand along my back as he fucks me, like I'm a beautiful sculpture he can't help touching while he rams his cock deep inside. This is my least favorite position, mostly because it was my ex's favorite—he liked to fuck me hard without having to look me in the face. I don't feel guilty thinking about my ex while Ree's cock is deep inside me—but it worries me. I've learned to listen hard to that gut instinct. It tried to tell me for months before the Massive Flameout that something was *wrong wrong wrong.* But I didn't listen. I thought I had it all, and I wanted to keep it too badly to let any little whisperings tell me something wasn't right. So I shut it out and let the man I loved fuck me like he didn't, and that should have been my warning signal all long. But Ree's not like Jeremiah. They're both white and male, but in every other way, they're polar opposites.

Yet my gut is saying *something*.

Ree's thrusting suddenly stops, and he's pulling me up from the table. His eyes are a little wide.

"Baby, you okay?" The words come out before I can think about them.

"Where were you?" he asks. It's a little panicked. Which I don't understand, but it makes my heart flutter, and not in a good way.

"I was on the table. Being fucked by you."

He swallows. "You were somewhere else."

I put a hand to his cheek and try to kiss him, but he moves his head and pulls back. It hurts, but I don't really understand what's happened. It hurts more when I realize: *he's never kissed me.* In all our lovemaking, all our rough-and-hard sex up against the rock wall in the bathroom or in his bed or bent over his couch, there was no actual kissing. The sweet and tender times, he brushed his lips across my cheeks, my nose, everywhere but my lips.

That's a fucking red flag if I've ever seen one.

Okay, gut, I'm listening now.

Ree rolls off the condom, pulls his pants back

up, and turns away. He drops it in the trash can hidden under the counter, then braces his hand against it, still not looking at me. I straighten up my clothes as well because it sure seems like we need to do less fucking and more talking. Or maybe I should just retreat to my room and let the man be. He doesn't owe me anything. Whatever we had going here was fun—no, it was fucking *hot*—while we had it. But he's saved my life. And my job. He's my "protection detail," and that's his job, and he does it damn well. He doesn't owe me anything more. And I'm not willing to be in *any* relationship with a man I can't trust—there's no compromise on that for me. Not anymore. I'll trust Ree with my life, but that doesn't mean I have to trust him with my heart.

He finally turns. "I'm not the kind of man a woman like you needs."

I arch an eyebrow. "I can decide what I need for myself, thank you very much."

His shoulders drop. "Of course you can."

"Then what's this about?" The man doesn't owe me, but any fool could see there's some dark torment roiling under all that rough exterior.

He sighs and takes my hand, leading me out of the kitchen and back to the couches. He's bent me over the back of said couches and spread me wide while hanging off them, but it looks like we're going to *sit* on those couches now. I take a spot, and Ree sits close, then seems to think better of that, scooting a little further away.

He's still holding my hand, although it's casual-like, just fingers laced across the back of the couch between us. "You were thinking of someone else. When we were at the table."

When we were fucking. But for some reason, Ree's suddenly tip-toeing around words. It's easy to guess that maybe he's been burned. I sure know a thing about that.

I give him a solemn nod. "I was. My ex-boyfriend-almost-fiancé."

"Ex?" Like he thinks maybe I'm still pining for Jeremiah.

Oh, hell no. "That boy's so far in my rearview mirror, he's in a different zip code."

Ree doesn't seem convinced. "Yet, you're thinking about him while I'm inside you."

"That is true." At the wince on his face, I hurry out, "But I'm not wishing it was him, Ree. I'm worried that this…" I gesture between us. "This hot and crazy thing we have going isn't really something you're into. *Like him.* Or maybe I've just been burned, and I'm a little skittish." I *don't* think it's that, but if he's been burned by someone, now's the time for him to fess up. I'm telling him straight-up I'm a little raw right now. He'll have to understand that and not be jumpy as hell whenever my mind wanders during sex. Or tell me what's on his mind. Either way.

"Did you really think I would just bed you and forget you?" he asks, but it's strained. He draws his hand back. "Did you think you're that kind of woman? The kind I could forget? Because you're not. You should know that."

"I don't know that." But his words heat my skin —that's the thing about Ree that's like no one else. *That intensity.* It burrows right into me and lights me on fire.

"I don't know what the hell your ex's problem was, but—"

"He fucked my best friend."

That stops Ree cold. He just stares at me a moment, so I tell him the rest. "We worked together. All three of us, at my prior job. Jeremiah and I started dating while we were all working long hours for our merger clients. I thought it was the real thing. He was a few years younger, but we had work in common, and all we did was work. We moved in together, and I thought for sure he saw marriage in our future. I know I did. We just needed to get through the next big job, maybe save up a little money. Then word came down they were going to promote someone in our group. I thought for sure it was me—I was lead, I had the most experience, and I was most requested by our clients. But no. They promoted Jeremiah to head of our division, and suddenly he was my boss. Which was fucking awkward enough, and I was pissed, but then I came home early one day and found him fucking my girlfriend—the other member of our team—in our bed."

There's fire in Ree's eyes. "Tell me you hurt him. Badly."

I huff a short laugh, but there's no humor in it. "That's when he fired me."

"What the fuck?" Ree's ready to murder something, and it makes my burned heart just a little glad.

"He made up some bullshit about me underperforming," I say bitterly. "Somehow, the problem was *me,* and I had to go. Suddenly, I was out of an apartment, lost a best friend and a boyfriend—well, good riddance there, fuck 'em—and had no job." I take a deep breath and let it out. "And then, just when I'd gotten a new job and almost moved on, the Vardigah came along. So when I said I needed to keep this job I have now, I really meant it, Ree. And you helped me do that, so…" I shake my head a little. "You don't owe me anything else, baby. If this thing between us isn't for you, it's okay. Just don't go fucking my best friend on your way out the door, okay?"

"That man was a coward." Ree's anger is still palpable, but there's relief behind it. Or maybe just a looseness I haven't seen on his face before.

"I think so." But that doesn't answer my question.

"I could destroy him for you if you'd like."

I laugh for real. But he's deadly serious. "That's not necessary. But thank you for the offer."

Ree bites his lip, and this is the most uncertain I've ever seen the man. He scoots closer and laces his fingers with mine again. "It's not that I don't want you, Jayda. It's that I'm afraid…" He blinks and presses his lips tight. "I'm not sure I believe in happy endings. Not for me, anyway."

I peer at him. *"That's* what you don't believe? Teleportation's fine. Magic healing, sure. But not that you could, what? Find someone to love?" But it feels right. The way he holds back. The way he's always too strong, in control—of everything and, if I'm honest, even me. Not in a terrible way. It's damn hot in the shower. But not so much in the relationship department. This is a man who thinks everything will fall apart if he lets go even a little.

"A woman like you needs a man who's not broken." He says it in all sincerity. It feels the closest he's ever come to opening up.

So I take a chance. "I'll tell you what I need." I slide my fingers away from his and rise up off the couch. Then I lift my blouse over my head and drop it on the floor. Ree's watching me with wide eyes. As I unhook my bra in the back, I tell him. "I need that big cock of yours." My bra falls to the floor. I bend down to slide my yoga pants off. "I need to ride it like I own it." Ree's eyes grow hungry. I reach for the stash of condoms he keeps in the table at the end of the couch—he has them all over the house. I'm sure he's had dozens of women he's fucked right here, but I'm also certain I'm the only one he's opened up to. The only one who knows what he needs—a woman who doesn't demand someone perfect, just someone decent. And Ree is the most decent man I've ever known.

In the time it's taken for me to get the condom and return, he's shucked off his shirt and pants and is waiting for me on the couch with the most glorious erection. I hand him the condom package and wait, standing over him with my hands on my hips, ready to take control of this man and his fears and turn them into something real—something he can *believe* in.

Once he's sheathed himself, I climb onto the couch and straddle him. Then I slowly lower myself, taking that enormous cock deep inside. "Oh, *fuck*," I breathe as I seat myself. I cradle his face between my breasts. His hands and tongue are already busy with them. I ease up and then ease down. "Are all dragons this big? Because *damn.*"

His hands slide down to my hips, where he grips me hard. "I'm the only dragon for you," he growls.

I lift up and then slam back down.

"Fuck," he says into my chest.

"Is that right?" I ask as I slowly rise again.

"Yes," he pants, but his hands are loose on me again. He's letting me take control.

I ease back down, taking him all the way in, and stay seated for a second. My hands slide up into his hair, and I peer down at his dark eyes, all wide and scared. Of that happy ending? I'm not sure. But I want him to know he's in safe hands with me.

"Good thing you're my kind of dragon." I

brush my thumb across his bottom lip. "Tough. Tender. A *grown* man who knows how to take care of his business… and mine." I've got *all* his attention. I rise again until his cock almost slips out. "Now, prepare yourself. Because I'm going to fuck you, Ree, all the way to that happy ending." I slam down on him, and he cries out. I brace my hands on his shoulders, pinning him back on the couch, and get serious about riding this man's cock. Up and down, quickly ramping up the pace, until he's a rock-hard joystick that I'm taking all the way home. He's grunting and whimpering with every slam down, and *Lord,* do I love that manly pleasure music he's making. I feel the quiver build deep inside me, a flutter with each bang down on his luscious cock. Ree's gaze is focused on my breasts bouncing in his face.

"Yes, please, yes," he begs, and I love the sound of that.

I go at him even harder, but then he slides one of his hands between us, and now he's flicking my nub with each pass, and *oh shit,* that's getting me there fast.

"Ree!" I gasp. I can't last this way.

He jerks up into me. "I'm going to—" Then he grabs my body, holding me tight while he gushes inside me. That deeply sexy feeling reverberates through me, and I come and come, shaking and squeezing that giant cock. A long, low groan rumbles through his body as he shudders and releases. *"Fuck. Yes,"* he breathes, but it keeps going, for both of us, for a while. When the aftershocks finally subside, he slumps back against the couch, head tipped to the ceiling, eyes closed. "Holy fuck, Jayda."

"Was that ending happy enough for you?" I tease, breathless as well.

He just lies there, sated.

I lean forward, breasts pressed against him, his softening cock still deep inside me. I take his cheeks in my hands, and he lifts his head, eyes drunk with sex, as he lazily opens them.

So I kiss him.

Full on the mouth, my lips asking permission, but not waiting for an answer before my tongue dives in, exploring the hotness of this man. He's shocked by it, his hands suddenly on me, like he will push me away, but then he doesn't. He lets me lavish this kiss upon him, and a moment later, he returns it. His tongue tangling with mine, his hands sliding up and going deep in my hair, not trying to move me to his will, just luxuriating in the feel of it.

I can hear his breath quicken, and it *is* a damn hot kiss, but there's something more—something connecting between us that's cracking open my bruised heart. My gut is saying, *Let this man in,* and I tell it, *I've already got his cock buried in me,* but the gut is right. I've got to let him all the way in.

Then Ree takes control, but only enough to pivot us down on the couch. He slides his cock from my body, and I miss that connection, but now he's on top of me, kissing me hard, a different connection which feels even deeper.

When he pulls back and stares down at me in wonder, those hard eyes of his are glistening.

It reaches inside me and wrenches my heart. I touch his face with my fingertips. "Who hurt you, baby? Tell me, so I can destroy them." But that seems the wrong thing to say because the tears just come harder, almost ready to break loose. "Shhh." I run my fingers across his lips. "You don't have to say it."

He leans back, jaw setting hard, eyes wide.

Something on the floor buzzes. It's his phone, buried in his track pants pocket. He disengages from me completely and sits up on the couch, but before he can dig out the phone, it stops buzzing and starts to ring. He scrambles to extract it from the pocket.

"It's from Niko," he says, his expression still shook.

He takes the call.

EIGHT

Ree

_____

Niko is shouting in my ear.

"Slow down," I say. "Start over." My brain is still reeling from the mind-blowing sex with Jayda. My heart is exploding with the things she's said. But most of all, it's the kiss. *A True Kiss.* The thing I've been desperately trying to avoid, but Jayda just opened her heart and pulled me right in. It's everything the fairy tales about soul mates have ever described—a connection so deep and so true it can't be anything but your other half bonding with you across magical space.

I thought I could have her—taste her, fuck her, enjoy everything about her—without risking the mating. Without falling in love. Without making that fateful connection. Then it wouldn't hurt so bad when I lose her. Because that's what my heart knows would happen. That's how life—*my* life—works. I told myself I could get away with it, but even that's a lie—I knew I'd never stay away from her. And when I lose her, to the Vardigah or when she simply decides I'm too broken, too fucked up to keep, it will kill me. Maybe not outright, but that's a possibility too. Dragons *do* die from broken hearts. All the fucking time. But even if I don't wither away, she's my last and only chance, my one and only soul mate. Losing her will shatter everything inside me. I've known it instinctively, all along, deep in my bones.

Niko's jabbering on again. *Fuck. Focus, Ree!*

"—so you've got to search everything."

Shit. What is he talking about? "Niko, I've got a bad connection here. Can you repeat that?"

"Are you okay?" he asks.

No. "I can hear you better now."

Niko sighs. "Look, we think we've figured out how the Vardigah are tracking the soul mates."

I straighten up. "How?" I look to Jayda—the sweet concern on her face, which was cracking open my heart even before that True Kiss, has me reaching a hand over to hold hers.

"A couple other soul mates have had their

houses ransacked," he says. "We almost lost one, but she held him off with a seventh-century Ottoman sword."

"Of course, she did." My heart is soaring. Because eliminating this threat is everything. "But what was the connection between them?"

"Every one of them still had something from their time in the Vardigah's torture cells. Could be as simple as their clothes. One kept a bracelet. Grace had her red shoes. You need to ask Jayda—did she have anything in that alley that also traveled to the Vardigah realm? If so, that seals it. And you need to get rid of it immediately."

"Okay, hold on." I lift the phone away and briefly explain it to Jayda.

Her eyes go wide. "The shoes. Prada. I was wearing them in the alley."

To Niko, I say, "I've got confirmation. Her shoes in the alley were the same as when she was kidnapped." I'm fucking kicking myself for bringing those back from her apartment.

"Copy that." He breathes out audibly over the phone. "I think that's it. The soul mates who threw out everything—shoes, jewelry, clothing—that reminded them of the torture haven't had the

Vardigah find them. Purge anything left over, and I think you're safe."

"I might need transport to do that." I glance at Jayda, but she's got the same hopeful look that's lifting my heart.

"Just text me. I've got every mated dragon working the others. I'm your direct contact."

"Copy that." I sigh. "And thanks. That's good news."

"Yeah. *Finally.* Talk soon." Niko hangs up.

I put the phone down. "You left those shoes back in the alley, right?" Jayda nods to confirm. "Do you have anything else? Bracelets? Earrings? Even underwear? The Vardigah track *things.* We need to make sure there's nothing left."

"I threw everything else out. I'm sure of it."

Relief trickles through me. I squeeze her hand. "Good." I suck in a breath. So much has shifted in just a few moments. I need to get my bearings. I don't know what this means for *us.* "You're safe now," I say, starting with what I know. I check the time. "It's ten o'clock, but that's only four p.m. New York time. If you're sure everything's clear from your apartment, there's no reason you have to stay here." At her small frown, I quickly add, "Of course, there's no reason you have to move back right away, either." *Shit,* that didn't sound any better. "It's up to you."

My heart is in freefall. She's safe from the Vardigah—but there's no guarantee on my second-biggest fear. That she'd want nothing to do with someone as fucked up as me. That if she knew me —not just as her protection detail, but as her soul mate—she'd run screaming back to her high-powered career and life in New York City and count herself lucky to have gotten out while she could.

"Oh. Well." She seems uncertain. "I suppose I should go home."

"Sure." But it stabs me. I'm still naked from her riding me on the couch. Her clothes are in a pile on the floor. She lifts the pieces out. I scoop mine off the couch and stand. "I'll start packing your things." There's almost nothing to pack, but I'm striding away from the couch anyway. I decide I need a shower, first—no idea why. But I toss my clothes on my bed and head straight in. The video feed's still there, and I can see she's stumbled into her bedroom and is heading for the bathroom.

I unplug it.

There's no reason for me to watch her every second now. The danger has passed—along with my reason for being part of her life. I step into the shower space and wave my hand at the sensor. I stand under the downpour for a full minute. What the fuck am I supposed to do now? Just let her go? She's everything I could want in a woman, even if we weren't literally two halves of the same soul. *Smart. Beautiful.* Taking her world by storm. I'm a fool to let that go. And I'm a fool to think she'll be satisfied with a knucklehead like me. Jayda's too smart to sign up for mating—being magically bound for all time to a man she barely knows? She'll take one look at that merger deal and say *Get the fuck out.* As she should. And then my life is fucking over because I'll never recover from that. I barely hold the pieces together as it is.

I should just let her go. I'll die unmated, but it's probably better that way. Better than taking a hit I know I can't survive. I soap up and work on convincing myself that's the best course of action. By the time I'm done, I'm not even sure how much time has passed.

Turns out a lot. That becomes clear when I return to the great room.

Jayda's waiting with her bags packed.

"I'll, um, text Niko." Which I do. My heart's hammering. *Fuck.* Am I just taking her home? Does she even want me to? Maybe I should just let Niko take her? *Oh, hell no.* I need at least a few more minutes with her, alone, to put this right—as right as it can be. Something's pricking the back of my eyes, and it takes until Niko shows up in my damn living room to figure out it's the same tears I was fighting off before. *Fuck. Me.*

I hold out my hand to Jayda while avoiding her eyes. She's got her stuff—the computer bag over her shoulder and her duffle in hand.

"Ready," I say to Niko.

He's giving me an odd look, eyebrow arched like he wonders what the fuck I'm doing. As if I know. But he says nothing, just teleports us to Jayda's apartment. I've been here before, of course, when I was gathering up her things. Poked through a lot of her stuff, like an asshole. She's got a decent apartment in Midtown, which is no small feat—she must make enough on her high-flying corporate salary to support the quality, understated furnishings. There's even a small view. If I thought material things mattered to her, I could maybe offer her that—

dragons are good with money, and I've steered clear of the lairs for most of my life, which means I'm financially independent. The Euro lair is ostensibly my base, my connection to the dragon world, but I have apartments all over the globe. I could keep Jayda in style. She'd never have to work again.

But her work is important to her—and she's damn good at it.

There's nothing I can offer that she would want.

"You okay?" Niko asks again, this time in front of Jayda, who's putting her things down by the couch.

Fuck. I've been staring out the window. "Yeah. We're good. Thanks for the transport." I lift my chin, letting him know he can go.

He takes the hint. "All right. Call me if you need anything." He flicks a look at Jayda, who's busy with something in her computer bag. Then Niko teleports away.

Jayda turns once he's gone. "I know you've probably got places to go and things to do." She dips her head and gives me a serious look. "But before you run off, I've got a few questions."

"Questions?" I have no idea what she's after.

"About this dragon business."

"Oh." I blink then glance at the couch. "Do you want to sit down?"

"I was thinking the bedroom," she says with a straight face.

My eyebrows lift, and my heart lurches. One more fuck? I can't... no, I know I *can*... I just don't think I'll survive one last *goodbye fuck* with Jayda. And there's the remote chance that somehow we could mate. I can't take the chance of trapping her into that. She has a right to know the risks. "Bedroom, it is." Feels like accepting an execution order.

Jayda takes my hand then tows me toward the hall that leads to her bedroom. It's well-kept, sparsely furnished, just the bed, a dresser, and a desk that's obviously where she works at home. She leads me to the bed, perches on the edge, then pats the white comforter next to her.

I slowly ease down to sit.

She turns to face me more fully. "You've lived a long time, so I figure you know how all this works. And now that I've come to fully accept this magic business, I need to know a few facts."

"Fair enough." The sudden possibility of being *friends* looms over me. I'm not sure if my heart could take that either.

"First of all, this mating business." Her gaze is focused on me with that intensity she has.

I swallow. "Yes?"

"Grace mated with Theo, and now she can teleport. Said she could shift into a dragon as well. Is that true? And what else comes with that deal?"

"Yes, it's true. Also venom, super-healing, and longevity. Mated dragons live a long time."

Her eyebrows lift. "How long? You're already pretty long in years, old man."

A smile bursts on my face, then quickly fades. "A mated pair dies together—when one goes, the other passes. Their souls are joined, so that's just how it works. When they mate, the male's lifespan matches the female's, which is now enhanced with that super-healing magic. There's no set rule, but it's usually an extra hundred years longer than the normal human lifespan." I smile a little. "An *old* dragon like me gets the most out of the deal. I'd keep going as long as my mate." The smile dies with that. Because that's the fairy tale—the one I'm not going to have.

She frowns. "That's a pretty solid offer for both parties."

I shrug. "It only works if it works."

"What do you mean?" Her dark eyes are on fire in the way that always stirs me around.

I sigh, but she deserves to know all of it. "You can only mate with your soul mate. There's literally only one person on the planet this will work with. And just being soul mates isn't sufficient—you have to be *in love* and then you have to *make love.* There's a specific order to things. Once that's done, there's no undoing it. Your souls literally fuse. The transformation occurs, each of them coming into their dragon powers. There's no going back from that."

Her frown has deepened into a scowl. "And what happens if you don't?"

"Don't what?" I narrow my eyes. What is she getting at?

"You said if a dragon didn't mate, he would wither away and die. What about the female?"

Ah. "She just lives a normal life. When she dies, her dragon spirit will be reborn elsewhere. Her soul mate will have another chance to find her and win her heart." The last of that trails off. My heart's hammering again.

Jayda presses her lips together then drops her gaze to the bed between us. "But he might not make it that long. He might wither away before that happens."

"He might." A lump is gathering in my throat.

She shakes her head a little like there's some debate raging inside, and she's unwilling to back down. Then she lifts her gaze to meet mine again. "You should go after her. That's what's best for you, and for her, and well… I won't stand in the way of fate. But I want you to know, Mr. Personal Protection Detail, that I don't give a damn about any of that. I think you should be free to love who you love, and if it were up to me, I'd tie you up in my bed and keep you right here. Just so I could ride that fine-ass body of yours any time I liked."

My mouth is hanging open. I couldn't be more stunned if she'd literally reached out and slapped me. "You… you'd like me to stay," I manage to get out.

She levels a dead-serious stare at me. "I'm contemplating throwing you down on my bed and having my way with you one last time, regardless. Probably will regret it, if I don't."

A jittery feeling has started up, deep in my chest. "And after that?"

"I'd let you go after her." She gives a solemn nod. "Your soul mate's one lucky woman. She damn well better appreciate you, or I'll come kick her ass."

A weak laugh escapes me. But the jitter has seized hold of my heart. Here's my chance. I can walk away. She'll never know. She'll think I'm off living my life with someone else. She'll go on and find someone else, having a normal human life…

And that's as far as I get. Because the idea of Jayda with someone else short-circuits my brain. Not when there's a chance—literally any chance at all—that she might want me.

I reach for her hand and draw it up to my face. Turning her wrist up, I hold her gaze while I taste her, running my tongue on the delicate skin there and finishing with a kiss. "What if I told you I don't want to leave?"

Torment plays across her face. It makes my heart skip.

"You can't give up your life, Ree." She seems angry about this—not at me, but at a magical system she thinks will rob me of a long and happy life. "Besides, the fates think you should be with her, whoever she is."

I pull her closer and run my hand into her hair. Gripping there, I bring her in for a kiss. The kind I've wanted all along but never dared to take. It's just as hot as the first True Kiss, but half as long—

because I need to *speak*. "What if I told you the fates think I should be with you?"

"I'd say the hot sex has fried your brain." But she's breathing hard, lips parted, as affected by our kiss as I am. She cups my cheek with her hand. *"Ree,* dammit, I'm in love with you. Don't make this harder on me than it has to be."

A thrill shoots through me like nothing I've ever felt. I pull her hand from my face and gently push her onto the bed, on her back while I cover her luscious body with mine. My cock is already sprung. "Oh, I'm definitely going to make this *hard* on you." I grind into her, holding her arm above her head while I kiss her deeply. The connection is so pure, so tight, I already have a hard time telling where my body ends and hers begins, even though we're fully clothed.

When I finally break the kiss for air, her eyes are half-mast with lust. "Oh, *Lord,* I'm going to regret this, aren't I?" she breathes. But she's bucking into my rod-of-iron cock.

She still hasn't figured it out.

"Jayda, *ma moitié,*" I say, softly. "You're my soul mate."

She frowns up at me like I'm playing a terrible game with her.

I just laugh, hardly able to contain my smile. "You *are*. Why do you think I'm here?"

"Because you're my security… oh." She blinks a couple times as it settles in. "But…" She scowls and struggles to prop up on her elbows, forcing me to lean back and not crowd her so much. "Why didn't you *tell* me?"

I prop up beside her then run my hand over my face. "Because I'm a fucking mess? Because I couldn't bear to…" I struggle to say it out loud. "I don't believe in happy endings, remember?"

"That doesn't make any sense." She's spooling up to angry at *me* now. Which is probably fair—I haven't been straight with her about *this*. Anything but this. I've got guardrails and minefields set up around this topic for a reason.

I just have to tell her. "I was ten when the Vardigah came."

Her anger dissipates, and her eyes go wide. "Did they kidnap you?"

"They murdered my family. And everyone I knew."

She's aghast, of course, because it's not the kind of thing you tell people. Pretty much, ever. It's not something I have to explain to any dragon—most know that if you're from that time period, no one escaped unscathed. Humans, of course, know nothing about it. And I never got close enough to any of them for it to make a difference.

I take a deep breath and start. "My lair was in France. Not the estate where I brought you—that was a summer home—but not far from there. I had three brothers, my mother and father, five uncles— and that was just our family. It was a prosperous lair with large families and fairy-tale pairings where everyone was madly in love and had babies and more babies. Family was everything, *ma chérie*. I lost all of it when the Vardigah burned it to the ground. I was playing in the caves below the lair when they struck. I was buried down there for a week before it cooled enough to..." My voice catches. I work to clear it. "Before I could climb out over the ashes of my people."

"Oh, my God, Ree." She's turned on her side, too, peering earnestly into my eyes.

I have to look away. "I was a child. And being an orphan at that time... the world was not a kind place. Of course, I was *dragon*, so I could defend myself, but that didn't matter when all you really wanted was a home." I bring my gaze back to her. "As I grew up, I realized I would die an old and pathetic dragon because there was no way to find my soul mate. The fairy tales I lived with were destroyed in the fire. I made my peace with that long ago."

"Oh, baby." She places her hand over mine between us. "You could have loved anyone."

My smile feels like pain. "Ah, but it wouldn't have been this." I lift her hand to my lips and kiss the back. "I'd already seen the happy ending. I knew I wouldn't have *that*. Or a family. Human women cannot carry a dragon child unless they've been transformed, *ma moitié*. It would kill them. And I would outlive her by a hundred years. So, you see? Falling in love was never a very appetizing option." I take a deep breath. "And then suddenly, there was you. And you wanted nothing to do with my kind." I shrug one shoulder. "Understandable. But there was no happy ending for me there, either."

She's scouring my face, looking for more than I'm telling her. "But you took care of me."

I bite my lip. "You might not realize this, but you're pretty damn hot."

She gives me a look. "You did more than take me to bed."

The tightness in my chest returns. "Yes, I did. Despite my best efforts not to."

She frowns like she doesn't quite take my meaning.

"I didn't think the fairy tale could come true." The smile-of-pain is back. "Not for me. It never has, and I was convinced that, somehow…"

Her eyes go wide. "I'd send you away."

"Why would you want to bind yourself to a dragon for life?" It's hard to get the words out. "Being a soul mate got you kidnapped and tortured. Why would you ever love one of us?"

Her fingertips touch my cheek—I've never felt something so sweet. "Because you're fucking hot in bed."

I laugh, but it comes out tortured.

"And because you're the most decent man I've ever met." She leans forward and kisses me soft, on the lips.

I pull away, even though it's killing me. "I can't make love to you now." My heart's stuttering. "If there's any chance you actually love me, we might mate. And that bond is forever."

"I got that the first time you said it." She reaches for me again.

I stop her. "I don't think you understand. And you barely know me."

"*Ree.*" She scowls at me. "I want a grown man

who won't screw my best friend. I want a man who knows how to take care of me. I want someone who will stick around for life. Am I mistaken, or is that not exactly, precisely, what it means to be a dragon's mate?"

The high-flying feeling of hope is clashing with the raw terror in my chest. "Yes. That's exactly what it means."

"Then make love to me."

NINE

Jayda

Ree's kiss pushes me back *hard* into the bed.

It's like something is unlocked inside of him, and he's hungry for me in a way he hasn't been until now. And I thought I knew *desire* before. Ree's consuming my mouth while literally ripping the clothes from my body. Once he's yanked my yoga pants down and popped half the buttons off my blouse, he releases me from the torrent of kissing to stand up and fling off his own clothes.

"Side table," I pant, watching him undress with greedy eyes. The idea of having this gorgeous hunk of a man in my bed *forever*—faithful, bonded, mine for all time—is making me dizzy. "Condom."

He shoves down his pants and lurches to the side table, nearly ripping the drawer out completely.

I hustle to get my blouse and bra off before he can get the condom on. I barely make it. He's on me again, pushing me down on the bed while spreading my legs and positioning his cock at my entrance. We're both naked now, and the feel of his iron-clad muscles under my hands, his chest brushing my belly as he kisses his way up my neck, is the most delicious thing I can imagine.

In one swift stroke, he fills me.

If I weren't used to Ree's cock, I'd be crying out. Instead, I put my legs in the air and open up to take him, all while wrapping my arms around his head and whispering, "Fuck me, baby. So hard."

He groans, pulls back, and slams into me. I can't help the gasp then. He stays deep and bends to my ear. "You complete me, Jayda Williams." He pulls back and *thrusts* in. "Your soul is my soul." Another thrust. "Your heart beats with mine." Then he lifts up to look me in the eyes. "You are the greatest treasure I will ever have." He holds still now to kiss me, so sweet and tender, I want to cry. But even more, I want him to *move*. Because this wide-open spread has him so deep inside me, I feel like he's filling up my soul, not just my body. I reach down to that fine ass of his and urge him on. He pulls back and strokes in, smooth as silk, no rush, just the long slide of his cock into my body. Like he's built just for me. The perfect man, the perfect cock—even the doubts that brought him nearly to tears are perfect. Because I know how to give a man all the love he can handle—I just need one I know can handle it. And who will love the hell out of me every which way in return.

Ree is that and so much more.

"I want this to last forever," he whispers, voice strained as he methodically strokes into me.

"That's what this is, baby. Forever."

"I mean *this.*" He peers down between our bodies and thrusts a little harder.

"If you want to fuck me endlessly, you'll get no argument from me."

But he's all sweetness and light. "I want this moment to last forever," he whispers as he dips his head down by mine. He grabs my ass and tilts me up, just enough to somehow go deeper.

"Baby, I am not going to last forever if you keep doing that."

But he keeps going, slow and steady. "I want this moment to stay, right here, before you're mine for all time." His voice is shaking. "Just in case."

The darkness is still there for him. And as much as I wish my words would banish it, I know he won't believe it until it's done. Hell, I won't believe half of it even after it's done. The whole thing is insane. But I want him to hurry up and get to that other side.

So I dig my fingers into his shoulders and say, "Fuck me like you mean it, Ree. Like you want to give everything to me."

He makes a small noise, something like a whimper, but then he's hooking his arms under my legs and pulling them up to my shoulders and slamming his cock so hard, I yelp. He's pistoning into me now, making all those manly groans, as if he's made of sex energy, and he wants to bang it into me by sheer force. We're bouncing the bed, and each thrust is climbing me higher. "Yes, baby! Just like that!" I cry. "Give me all of it."

He groans and thrusts twice more then grinds into me. He's coming—I can tell by the way he writhes, and it rubs me just the right way, shoving me over the edge with him. I convulse, sweet pleasure rocketing through me. I buck up into him. "Oh, fuck, baby, fuck!" I cry out, the hot fullness of him inside me, the waves of orgasm all through me, it's heating me from the inside out. And this orgasm lasts and lasts. He's still twitching inside me, and mine keeps rolling on, wave after wave. He finally settles, but I'm burning up.

"Jayda," he gasps, and I think he's just riding the bliss, but then I realize my eyes are closed, and he's trying to get me to open them.

I blearily force my eyelids apart. He's hovering over me, concern etched on his face. His cock's still buried deep, and it feels so good… I can't imagine what's worrying him.

"It's okay, baby." I reach for his face, but my arms are all sweaty. "Jesus, we really did it, didn't we?" I'm still lazy with pleasure.

He wipes the sweat from my brow. "Are you okay? How do you feel?"

"I'm fine." I smile for him. "You burned me up."

It takes him a moment, but the concern slowly spreads into a smile. "I felt it, but I didn't quite believe…"

"Believe what?" I'm parched.

He leans in quick to kiss me. Then he grins. "We're mated. That's the transformation you're feeling."

"I'm pretty sure that's your cock I'm feeling." And sure enough, amazingly, the sex miracle that is Ree resurrects his cock, still deep inside me but quickly becoming just as stiff as when he was fucking me within an inch of my life.

He pulls out. I give a small sound of protest.

"Roll over," he says, and I do my best, but my limbs are all floppy from hot sex, and holy shit, the bed is soaked. Did I really sweat that much?

Just as I'm wondering that, Ree fills me again from behind. I'm lying face-down, prone on the bed, and he's positioned himself with that long cock sliding past my thighs and deep inside.

"Oh, *shit*, Ree," I say as he bottoms out. There's some magic happening between my legs. Like *literally*. Some electric shooting pleasure wherever his cock meets my hot, slick flesh, which is to say everywhere.

"You like that?" He pulls out then thrusts in, harder.

"Fuck!" A wave of that sparking pleasure sweeps through me.

He laughs softly. "Oh, we're going to do so much fucking." He thrusts hard again. *"Sweet magic,* I had no idea." Then he starts pistoning into me again, only this time, every stroke is like an electrical zap of magic. I'm shrieking with it, coming and coming, and I think I might actually pass out. Ree finally groans, long and deep, and holds me down to the bed, shuddering as he comes. He stays still like that a long time, emptying into me. As much as this round was *on fire*, my body is actually cooler now.

Ree slides out and collapses on the bed alongside me. I just lie flat for a while, still tingling everywhere. After a minute, his hand caresses my bottom, sliding up to my back. He brushes my hair away from my ear.

"You still alive over there?" His hand is winding my hair, playing with it.

I turn my head toward him and force my eyes to open. "Barely."

He's grinning—I don't think I've ever seen the man smile so wide.

I scoot a little, so I'm on my side, facing him. His cock is thick and heavy, but sated and soft for now. And then I notice…

"Hang on, what happened to the condom?"

"I took it off."

"You *what?*" I scrunch up my forehead.

He snuggles in, pulling my face to him, and kisses me. "*After* we were done," he explains. "But we don't need them anymore. We're mated."

"Okay." I guess it's official now. "What does that have to do with condoms?"

"It's difficult to get a mated dragon pregnant." He's stroking my breast, playing with the nipple at the end of each pass. "Could take years. Decades even."

"Wow." I blink and pay a little more attention to the sated but thoughtful expression on his face. He's licking his lips like he wants a taste of me. Before he gets too far with that… "Do you want babies?"

His gaze jumps up to mine. He's searching my eyes. "Yes." He's breathless, a little of that haunted look returning. "Lots. Lots and lots… Do you?"

"Well, I don't know about *lots.*" I hadn't given it any thought. "I mean, work takes up a lot of my time."

"I'll take care of them," he says quickly.

"Will you?" I raise both eyebrows. But the jarring question doesn't last long in my mind. I've never been so well-cared-for as when Ree was making sure I had everything I needed for safety, security, and success at work.

He's still breathing a little ragged. He slips his hand to my cheek, kisses me sweetly, then says, "If you give me a child, Jayda…" He stops and presses his forehead to mine. "You'll have given me *every-thing.*" He shudders, and I can hardly stand it.

How can this rough man be so sweet? I *want* to give him everything.

"Well, then." I run my hand down to that thick cock of his, stroking it softly to life. "We'd better get busy if we're going to make *lots* of babies."

He laughs a little, and it's filled with disbelief and joy. But he kisses me so tenderly, I know without any doubt, he would be the world's most amazing father. And the idea of giving Ree a *family*… well, that idea's quickly growing on me.

Which is a good thing because the first time he takes me with no condom, I'm just sure that manly seed of his is getting me pregnant already.

TEN

Ree

2 AM—TIME TO PLAY.

We're on New York time for Jayda's job, and it's 8 pm there, which means she'll be home any minute. I've turned down any new assignments for the duration. Too much to do. *I'm honeymooning.* Something I never thought possible. Beyond work and simple survival, I've spent my entire adult life chasing after sex. It's not like I didn't *know* I was trying to fill a void that couldn't be filled—I was making the best of the fate I'd been given. But all that sexing didn't prepare me for the joy of being mated. The magical sex enhancement, a pleasure boost every time I touch Jayda, is fucking outstanding, but it's far more than that. It's finding my other half. It's knowing we'll be together until the literal end. It's building a life around that simple, pure, amazing fact.

I'm fixing up the estate—it's my ancestral home, and it's where I want to raise our kids. The Euro lair is fine, but not very family-oriented. Although that may be changing soon with everyone paired up with their soul mates. Depends on whether they can seal the deal. That I think in family terms now is another astonishing fact. But I fucking love it. Our kids, whenever they come, will have everything I had, when I was younger, and everything I didn't, once it was all taken from me.

Family. It's only been a week, and I still wake up in a cold sweat sometimes, afraid the Vardigah have come to rip it all away. Niko says they can't find us —they won't destroy this dream-come-true I'm having. But it's only Jayda in my bed, her warm brown skin soft against my hands, that slows my raging pulse and soothes my panic. That she could come to love me, as broken as I am, with such astonishing speed, tells me I've finally found the fairy tale ending. *It's real*—and I'm wrenching the joy out of every minute of it.

I'm waiting in our bedroom at the estate's apartment for her to arrive. She usually teleports straight from the elevator, assuming it's empty and she can get away unnoticed. The estate is much larger than these small quarters into which I've sequestered myself whenever I was here. I'd only acquired the property a hundred years ago. After my family was destroyed, the estate was taken over by a local nobleman. It suffered from neglect over the years, and even when I managed to buy it back, I couldn't bring myself to resurrect it to its former glory. Over the decades, it fell into even further disrepair, very much resembling the haunted castle it felt like to me. In the last decade, I remodeled this small corner—the apartment—so I could use the property to some extent. One of the many temporary "homes" I kept around the world. I'm selling off most of those now, keeping a few so we'll have places to stay when we travel. I'm investing everything into making a home for Jayda and me.

And our children, when they come.

Jayda arrives, teleporting out of thin air.

"Hello there, gorgeous." I pull her into a quick kiss, then relieve her of her laptop bag.

"You would not believe Arnie today." Her shoulders are dragging down.

I scowl as I set aside her work bag. "Is he ogling you again? Because I'd be happy to make an encore visit as your bodyguard and scare the hell out of that guy."

She sighs. "No, he's just questioning all my numbers again. They're getting ready to launch the acquisition team, and it's like he's never looked at the due diligence report."

I give her another quick kiss. "So he's an asshole who can't keep up and is slowing everyone else down."

"Maybe. It's just frustrating to have to go over everything *again.*"

I slide my arms around her waist and pull her close. "I'm an expert at relieving frustration."

A tiny smile lights up her face. "Is that right?"

I dip my head to nibble on her neck. "If they granted PhDs in giving orgasms, I should get at least a few honorary degrees."

"Mmm," she says as I taste her. "I could be your thesis advisor if you'd like."

"Does this mean I'll have to give an oral exam?" My hands are already under her blouse, working at her bra clasps.

"Oh, baby, I've been thinking about that all day."

"Well, then." I reach to the bottom of her skirt and hike that up. I waste no time getting her panties off and backing her up against the dresser. I hook her legs over my shoulder and dive in, tongue first.

"Oh, *fuck*, Ree." Her hands dig into my hair, and she's squirming under my touch. During the daytime in New York, the office has her, body and mind, but when she's home here in France, I want every part of her to myself. Given the gasps and cursing right now, I'd say I have her full attention. The first orgasm is almost too easy. The magic sparks off my tongue, and I'm getting better at using that to maximum advantage. When she stops convulsing, going deliciously soft against me and the dresser, I come up for air, shove down my pants, and quickly get inside her. *"Yes,"* she breathes, taking me all the way in. "Do you know I daydream about your cock?"

I pull back slow then thrust in hard. *Fuck.* "I spent an hour in the shower after you left this morning." I thrust again. God, she's so tight. So perfect.

She laughs a little, breathless. "Were you *very* dirty?" She's playing with my hair as I rock the dresser with how hard I'm fucking her.

"I kept thinking about you," I pant as I thrust. "I had to beat off three times. Or else I'd walk around with a hard-on all day. And I've got remodeling to do."

"*Oh,*" she says as I tip her back, angling deeper.

"*Yes,*" I breathe while I thrust, the magic ripping along my cock. "Take all of me." And then I shut the fuck up because we're both getting close, banging the dresser against the wall and cursing our way to a simultaneous orgasm that blows my mind. There's something about the magic there too—it syncs us up. Or maybe it's just that it feels so damn good, we can't help racing to climax together. But I'm shooting off and groaning into her shoulder as she cries out and bucks into me. It fucking lasts too —like three orgasms strung together, just going and going.

Fuck, mated sex is hot.

I'm panting when it's done, and Jayda looks wiped. I know she'll bounce back, but she gives her all at the office then comes home, and I'm on her from the jump. Not that she doesn't want it, but it's quite the pace. Especially since we can spend half the night buried in each other, and before we know it, she's got to get back over there. And tonight I have something special.

"Shower," I say.

"Oh, baby, I don't think I'm ready for more." Her eyes are half-closed.

I grin. "I mean the kind with soap and no fucking."

Her eyes blink open. "Really?"

I laugh—a real, full-body chuckle; I've had more reasons to laugh in the last week than the whole ten years prior—and then I lead her to the bathroom. I make her stand still while I soap her up and get her all squeaky clean. Then I shoo her out of the spray and tell her to go get dressed. I have to quickly beat off—my soul mate is hot, and it just can't be helped—but then I'm out and ready to show her what I've been working on all day.

I hold out my hand for her to take, which she does. Just the touch of her makes me happy. It's insane. "Okay, close your eyes," I say. "I have a surprise."

"Where are we going?" Because of course, we're teleporting.

"You'll see."

She dutifully closes her eyes, and I transport us to the south tower. Both the south and west towers overlook the river, with a grand walkway between. The estate is mostly an enclosed courtyard area with several levels of rooms in the walls surrounding it. The south tower is the most picturesque and faces away from the small village nearby.

"You can open your eyes now," I say.

She does, and they go satisfyingly wide. I've cleaned up the top level of the tower, accessible only by a stone spiral staircase up the narrow column. The stone flooring has several carpets overlaid, there are fresh windows in the stone frames, and I've built in a child-sized play castle on one side and a small stage on the other, complete with curtain for performances. A string of miniature lights runs along the edge of the ceiling around the entire circular perimeter of the room. The doors to the stone balcony are thrown open—there's no moon tonight, only the soft glow of the lights on the parapet outside.

"Where are we?" She gives the miniature castle a strange look. "And you realize we don't have children yet, right?"

I grin and come up behind to hug her. "I keep trying. Give my magic dragon sperm a chance."

She laughs softly and cradles my arm. "It's beautiful, Ree."

"Come outside with me." I take her hand and lead her to the balcony. It's two in the morning, so there aren't any lights in the village, and even the hanging lamps over the bridge have been turned half off for the night. I'd previously placed a couple glasses and a bottle of champagne on the waist-high stone wall—I snatch them up and pour.

"What are we celebrating?" She takes the glass and sips.

"A week of being mated."

She raises her glass and clinks it with mine. "May all our weeks be filled with this much sex."

I tip my glass to her. "I'll get to that in a moment."

"Oh, will you?" She grins and takes a longer sip.

I set my glass down and slide up behind her, turning her toward the parapet edge, looking out over the darkened village. "No moon tonight," I say.

"Are we going to fly?" She squeezes my arm around her waist and drains her drink faster. She loves flying, but we can't often take the chance of being seen. Moonless nights in the south of France are a good time for it.

"There's something I want to ask you first."

"Yes, I absolutely want to have more sex tonight."

I pull her hair to the side so I can nuzzle her neck from behind. "That wasn't it. But yes."

"No, you may not turn the entire estate into a playground for kids we don't even have."

"But I've already got the plans drawn up!" I'm grinning behind her ear.

"It's not practical."

I give an elaborate sigh. "Well, all right then."

She drinks the last of her champagne and sets the glass down. "Okay, what did you want to ask me?"

"Will you marry me?" I say it simple because that's what it is.

She jolts and then turns in my arms, but there's no light to see in the shadows out here. "We're mated, Ree."

"I know. It's fantastic." I slide my hands under the loose cotton t-shirt and down into the yoga pants she's changed into.

She faces forward again. "I suppose getting married would make things easier. Legally speaking."

I nuzzle into her hair. "I want to marry you because I love you."

"Well, there's that, too." But I can hear the smile in her voice.

"So, that's a yes?"

"You drive a hard bargain."

I slip my hand between her legs. "Driving hard is something I do well."

"Ree, we're outside." But her body's not objecting. I slide her pants down and mine as well. Then I bend her over, her hands gripping the stone as I take her from behind. "Fuck," she breathes, leaning back into my stroke. *"Ree."*

"I'm sorry." I grip her hips so I can thrust like I want to. "You did say *drive me hard,* didn't you?"

"Yes, Oh, God, Ree, *yes!*"

"That's what I want to hear." But it's strained because I'm rocketing there fast. I don't know if it's the magic sizzling along my cock or the fresh night air or the fact that I'm potentially making a baby right here, right now, with the woman I love beyond all reason… but I'm about to explode. "Say you'll marry me, Jayda," I pant.

"Yes! I will marry you. Fuck, Ree!"

And then I bring us both home. Twin orgasms welling up and shaking us both, cursing and clenching the parapet while we come. It takes a while to finish and even longer to come down. There's no hurry, and nowhere I'd rather be. Eventually, the cool night air reminds us to disengage and actually pull our clothes on. She wants to go fly, but I'd like to just cuddle for a moment. That's something new as well—snuggling was never high on the list when I was fucking my way across the world and through time, always making up for the things I couldn't have. Now, with Jayda, my entire world is right here in my arms.

"Are we going to fly before sleeping? Or sleep and then fly?" Her voice is soft, and I hear the fatigue in it. We need to catch up on sleep sometime soon.

"Maybe just a quick flight tonight. If you sleep, it'll be light before you know it." The timing is all off, living both in New York and France, but it's worth it—it's the best of both worlds, for her and for me.

She nods against my chest.

Before we can shift and get to it, my phone buzzes in my pocket. I consider letting it go, but something nudges my brain to take a look.

"It's Niko," I say with a frown.

"What does he want?"

"To talk—wants to visit." I don't like it. "Why don't you go for a quick flight around the estate? I'll see what he wants."

"You don't want to come?"

"No, you go ahead."

She shrugs off her clothes, and I step back to give her room. She shifts into her midnight black dragon form, as beautiful in that as she is when

145

human, then she leaps into the air, spreading her wings and taking flight. She's as dark as the night around her, so I quickly lose her as she glides on the air currents curling around the estate.

I text Niko back. *Come on over.*

He appears a moment later. "Hey, sorry to interrupt…" He looks around, but Jayda's dragon is long gone.

"What's up?" I ask. Not to rush him or anything, but I only get Jayda during certain hours of the day.

"Everything all right here?" Niko's concern hikes up substantially.

"Yes? Jayda will be back soon." Now *I'm* concerned. "What is this about?"

"You remember Jayda and Grace's friend, Daisy? Well, she's waking up."

My eyebrows lift. "I thought she was in a coma."

"She was." Niko shakes his head. "Is? Maybe? Akkan's by her side pretty much constantly. He says she's talking, but she's not awake."

"Talking in her sleep?" I'm not sure why that's a huge concern—although I'm sure Jayda will be glad to hear about any progress with her friend.

"More like a fever dream. It's what she's *saying*

that's concerning." Niko shrugs, but it looks tense. *"The shadow and the light. There can be no peace."*

"If she's feverish, why does it matter what she says?"

Niko scowls. "She says *they're coming.*"

"Who?"

"The Vardigah." He winces. "She's not awake, Ree. She's not conscious. But she's *warning us.*"

I stare at him. It's not enough to get concerned about. It's hardly anything at all. But Niko's led his lair for two hundred years and is almost solely responsible for the rescue of the soul mates from the Vardigah's clutches—including Jayda. I brought her back, but he's the one who made it happen. I trust his gut instinct on almost anything. And I can't afford to take chances.

"I'll tell Jayda," I say. "Maybe a visit will help bring Daisy back."

Niko clasps a hand to my shoulder. "Thank you, my brother."

My brother. It's a common thing to say among dragons. There are so few of us left. But it's never really felt right until now.

Niko disappears, teleporting away from the dream-come-true I'm having with my one-and-only soul mate.

The chill night air makes me shudder.

Please don't let this be anything, I send up a fervent prayer to the Universe. A cold and cruel Universe that's never listened to my prayers before.

Then I shift out of my clothes and into my dragon form and leap into the air.

I need to find my mate and keep her safe.

Jayda and Ree have their HEA... but can they keep it? And will Daisy ever wake up? Find out in the next Broken Souls story, *My Dragon Master* (Broken Souls 6).

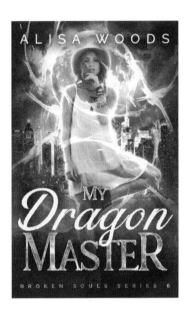

Get My Dragon Master today!

Subscribe to Alisa's newsletter

for new releases and giveaways

http://smarturl.it/AWsubscribeBARDS

About the Author

Alisa Woods lives in the Midwest with her husband and family, but her heart will always belong to the beaches and mountains where she grew up. She writes sexy paranormal romances about complicated men and the strong women who love them. Her books explore the struggles we all have, where we resist—and succumb to—our most tempting vices as well as our greatest desires. No matter the challenge, Alisa firmly believes that hearts can mend and love will triumph over all.

www.AlisaWoodsAuthor.com

Printed in Great Britain
by Amazon

38687409R00095